A Love Like His

J.D. Parks

Parks Publishing & Consulting Company, LLC

ISBN -13: 978-1-7326967-7-8

Editing by: Jalesa Parks

Front cover image: Shutterstock images

Print services provided by KDP
United States of America
First printing: September 2020

Published by Parks Publishing & Consulting Co, LLC
P.O. Box 66
Olive Branch, MS 38654

He who finds a wife finds a good thing and obtains favor from the Lord.

-Proverbs 18:22, NIV

Prologue

She had heard enough. Snatching her toiletries from the dresser, she stormed out of the bedroom to put as much distance between them as possible for fear that she might say something she would later regret, truly crushing his pride.

And yet again, she thought rolling her eyes, *here I am taking his feelings into consideration even though he said everything he could to hurt me.* She chewed on her bottom lip anxiously, her mind reeling. He had spoken with such contempt and disdain that she felt like a piece of her had fallen off a shelf and broken into several pieces, and no matter how much she mulled over it, she couldn't quite pinpoint the moment that he had started feeling this way. She'd made a valiant effort to be the kind of woman he said he needed, supporting him to no end. All she knew was that today's activity had clearly awakened some resting demons in her husband-to-be, and she intended to get to the bottom of it if their future marriage would have a fighting chance.

"God, please, help us," she whispered, fumbling with the towel wrapped loosely around her petite frame. Tiptoeing to the community restroom, she hoped that the others hadn't heard them arguing. Compared to her relationship, the other couples seemed to be extremely ready for marriage. She couldn't confidently say that she was anymore, if she ever could. But she wanted to think that the foundation of her relationship could outlast any dilemma or disagreement that came their way. After all, they had been together for years, staying together through far worse; surely, one week couldn't ruin everything she had worked for.

She turned the shower knob to the far left, satisfied by the steam that began to rise, letting her know that it was perfect. After undressing, she slid behind the shower curtain and proceeded to wash her hair; the water passed softly through each strand and cascaded down her back. She envisioned her man's hands gliding down her stomach and resting on her hips. She knew that the mere thought was a sin and that the act itself would violate the promise she'd made to Pastor Moore, but what else was she supposed to do right now? It felt like forever since he had touched her affectionately, and she needed reassurance that he still wanted her just as much as she wanted him.

Or else— She shook her head vigorously, hoping to clear the doubt that never failed to rear its ugly head. No matter how hard she tried, it was always lurking in the distance, just waiting for an opportunity to destroy all confidence she had in herself and her relationship. *He loves me; I know he does*, she thought, running the soapy towel over her shoulders.

Just then, she heard the shower door slide open behind her. She wanted to leap into his arms because this would be a first. Even though they had verbally agreed to avoid sex during the retreat after nearly getting caught last time, the old adage "desperate times call for desperate measures," seemed to be at play, and she couldn't be happier that for once *he* had taken the initiative and joined her. Not to mention that he wasn't the type of man you told no, and she was desperate for reassurance. With her eyes closed, she relished in his touch as his arm snaked around her petite form while his hand roamed through her hair.

"Nice of you to join me," she whispered. Her body melted against him as she cupped his face, her eyes flying open in alarm.

Chapter 1

Maliah

Becoming a guidance counselor had been the greatest decision of Maliah's life. No, everyday wasn't blissful but days like today, when she watched her seniors walk across the stage, made it worth every hassle. Nearly all of them were either attending college or entering a trade program, which many of them had doubted would ever happen.

She fought back the tears that threatened to spring forward from her eyes, and as if on cue, Mike pressed his handkerchief in her hand. Maliah looked up at him with gratitude, clinging tighter to his chiseled arm. Even through his suit jacket, she could feel his hard work at the gym. His mocha brown, structured jawbone was lined with a slight stubble that added to his overall rugged appeal. His handsome features, along with his thoughtfulness, were the main reasons that she loved standing by his side. He exuded power and control without ever speaking. It was part of the reason that she had fallen in love with him so quickly. He had entered her life at a time when she felt utterly hopeless when it came to love. Mike made her feel and believe again. And now, they were engaged, and she couldn't be happier.

They had met two years ago at a single's mixer at the Melodies from Heaven Church of God in Christ. Maliah had been single for well over four years, and she had been talked into attending the mixer with her friend Jasmine, who had made it her personal goal to find Maliah a man as quickly as possible. Maliah had tried to come up with every excuse not to attend, but as usual, Jasmine showed up with an armful of make-up, garment bags, and heels, ready to tackle Maliah's doubt head-on, and it had worked.

Jasmine had snatched off the cape and turned Maliah around to look at herself in the mirror, and what she saw left her quite dumbfounded. She knew that Jasmine had skills, being a licensed cosmetologist and all, but the girl definitely had a way with her hands. She had practically worked a miracle on Maliah's dry natural curls, which now glistened with volume and shine. Even more, her skin had a new glow; her high cheekbones were accentuated with a golden bronzer, and smoky eyeshadow was layered on her dark, almond-shaped eyes. She couldn't deny that this new look was screaming sex appeal.

Jasmine had caught her smiling at herself and that further ignited the fire behind her mission. She had chosen a mustard yellow, knee-length bodycon dress for Maliah to wear with a pair of colorful, strappy heels. Maliah thought the dress looked very chic but far too revealing for her personality and size twenty-two body.

Sensing her apprehension, Jasmine grabbed the dress, walked behind her, and held it in front of her body. "Girl, look at how the color pops against your skin. It's e—verything," she said, snapping her fingers and smiling back at Maliah's puzzled reflection.

"I mean, Jasmine, it's a nice color, but it's very fitted. You know I don't typically wear dresses like this." She twisted to observe her physique from the side.

"And that's exactly what you need, ma-ma," she slapped Maliah's hip playfully before falling lazily on the futon. "You're not even thirty yet, Liah. You have to stop wearing these old church suits and stuff. It ages you." She popped open her compact mirror, examining her lipstick.

Maliah frowned at her, before picking up a couch pillow and tossing it at her. "Well, thanks for telling me I have no style!"

Jasmine caught the pillow. "I didn't say that. You get it right a lot of the time, but for some reason, teachers and church folk think they gotta dress all prim and proper. That's boring. And there is absolutely nothing boring about you." She sat up, crossing her legs at the knee. "Believe me. If you were boring, we wouldn't even be friends."

"Hmm, thanks," Maliah snorted. "Maybe I'll try it on and see how it looks then."

Jasmine jumped up excitedly. "That's a start!" Once again, Jasmine had been right. The dress had tastefully displayed every curve, and Maliah had found herself feeling quite feminine and sexy. The dress hugged her hips and punctuated her round bottom with great precision. And when she'd slipped into the heels, she had felt like an instant winner. Add her shoulder-length hair with honey brown highlights and a pop of fuchsia lipstick, and she had been ready to mingle.

Apparently, the dress had worked like a charm because that night she'd met Mike Peterson. He had been the fourth guy to sit down at her table. While the others had seemed slightly threatened by her educational achievements, Mike had arrived with accomplishments of his own. Like her, he was in the world of education and devoted much of his time as an assistant principal at Hollow Oaks Middle School. Ironically, Maliah worked as the guidance counselor at Hollow Oaks High. Even funnier was the fact that they attended the same church; however, she came during the 8:00 service while he visited for the 11:00 session. Therefore, they had never ran into each other.

They had spent the first part of their meeting discussing their jobs and career aspirations, but they quickly realized they had several other things in common. Neither of them had children, pets, or ex-spouses. They had both recently purchased their first homes, and they were currently enrolled in doctoral programs. More importantly, they were both looking to find love and get married sooner rather than later.

Before Maliah knew it, Pastor Charlotte Moore

stood in front of the singles and announced that the mixer was coming to an end. Maliah was surprised by the feeling of disappointment that suddenly rested on her shoulders. Even though she had been conversing with Mike for the past two hours, she hated to admit that she didn't want the night to end.

As if reading her mind, Mike turned to her, a grimace etched across his face. "I don't want to be too forward," he said softly, "but I gotta admit that I'm really enjoying our time together. Can I take you to Le Soiree? It's a small bakery just up the street. It doesn't close for another two hours." His eyes pleaded to her, seeming to peer deep into her soul.

Surely he knows that I want to go, she thought. "I've enjoyed meeting you tonight, too, Mike," she said, placing her hand on top of his. "But I must decline. I have to be at the school early tomorrow morning. I'm afraid that long nights and early mornings aren't good for me." She laughed nervously, hating to be the bearer of bad news.

His head lowered in disappointment. "Y-yeah, yeah. I'm sorry. I forgot that we both have to be up tomorrow, huh?" He chuckled nervously. "Well, can I get your number? I would love to take you out this weekend." He offered her a devilish smile, making it clear that he wasn't going to take no for an answer.

"Sure, and yes, I'd love to see you this weekend." She pulled out her phone and smiled up at him.

They had swapped numbers, and as promised, he had called her the next day to set up their date. The date was filled with small surprises and steady compliments. Even more, their conversation had continued to flow effortlessly, the night ending with Maliah breaking one of her rules, which was to never kiss on the first date. And since then, they hadn't stopped kissing.

"You ready to go, baby?" Mike cupped her elbow, staring at her inquisitively.

Maliah tore her dazed eyes away from the large group of students taking pictures with their family and friends and smiled up at him. "Yeah, let's go." She wrapped her arm about his waist while readjusting her purse on her shoulder. "Think we can stop by Le Soir—"

Her words were cut short by a smirking, Camilla Johnson, a tall, scrawny and former-beauty queen who worked as a librarian at Hollow Oaks High by day and trolled for any man she could sink her desperate claws into by night. Unfortunate for

Maliah, those claws had once been deep in Mike, as he and Camilla had dated for over two years before he had met Maliah. And from the way Camilla was eyeing him right now, she intended to come back for seconds, regardless of his relationship with Maliah.

"Hi Mr. Peterson," she drawled, darting her eyes quickly in Maliah's direction but decidedly dismissing her. "Ms. Jamerson," she said sharply, reverting her attention back to Mike. "I know you are so pleased with these students. You met most of them as sixth graders at the middle school." She swatted his arm, clearly hoping to get a rise from Maliah.

Maliah rolled her eyes, still holding Mike's arm and glancing at her watch.

Mike shifted his weight uncomfortably from one foot to the other. "Yeah, these used to be my kiddos. You all did a very good job keeping them on course." He looked down at Maliah. "But if you will excuse us," he said, stepping out of Camille's reach and ushering Maliah forward by her hand, "we have somewhere to be before it closes." He held Maliah's hand close to his chest while offering her a reassuring wink.

They strolled out of the convention center,

leaving a gawking and fuming Camille standing in the middle of the hall, their steps, hearts, and minds in sync, and Maliah knew she had been blessed with the man of her dreams. She could not wait to marry him in six months.

Chapter Two

Alyssa

"Guys, get down! Please, Get down!" Alyssa yelled, a migraine threatening to immobilize her as the boys teeter-tottered from one barstool to another. Keith's sons had only been with them for three days, and she was already looking forward to their departure in two weeks. KJ was seven-years-old and obsessed with video games and jumping from couch-to-couch while his partner-in-crime was a busy and extremely talkative three-year-old named Dylan, who loved reminding Alyssa that she wasn't his mother.

Alyssa hated to admit that being their mother full-time was the last thing she wanted. They, clearly, lacked the home-training and discipline that she had been raised on, and she didn't know how to get Keith to see it. All of her concerns were defended by the 'boys will be boys' mantra, but they were destructive, disrespectful, and entitled little beasts of burden that she could live without. But, for Keith, she would tolerate them. After all, over the past year and a half, Keith Seymore Woodward had made her happier than any man in her life.

The sound of glass shattering snapped her out of her reverie; she ran towards the sound, spotting the boys sitting quietly on the couch in the living room, the fallen vase lying at their feet. Alyssa stifled a loud groan, realizing it was the vase her sorority sister had given her as a housewarming gift. Standing with her hands nestled on her hips, she looked from the broken vase to the two boys, who stared at the television blankly, pretending that they were too immersed in the program to notice her glare. But she could see Dylan looking at her out of the corner of his eye.

"Who did this?" she asked, her voice coming out calmer than she actually felt. Inwardly, her heart was pounding with frustration and anger. "I said, who did this?" she asked again through clenched teeth, her fists balled up by her side.

The boys ignored her, continuing to stare at the screen, sometimes looking at her pointedly before turning their attention back to the cartoon show.

Unsure of her next move, Alyssa grabbed the broom and dustpan, sank to her knees, and swept up the glass pieces, stress rolling down her back as she dumped them into the garbage can. She could feel an onslaught of tears coming; it had clearly been building up over the past two days. Luckily, the boys were still watching T.V. so they hadn't seen her all emotional, but she wasn't sure if she could deal with all of this for another day.

This was the second valuable item they had broken. She understood that kids were clumsy, but they were just all out reckless, and even worse, she had decorated the house without regards for a kid-friendly environment because Keith had assured her that his children were well-behaved, and now, she felt her mother's words creeping back into her mind: *Baby, that man has too much baggage for you. You're too young to have to deal with all that. Trust me; I know.*

Alyssa rolled her eyes as she sauntered into her bedroom, closing and locking the door behind her. Yes, there was a ten-year age difference between her and Keith, but he made her feel more secure than anyone she had ever met before. *Surely, her mother, of all people, could understand*, she thought, flopping onto the bed.

Prior to Keith, Alyssa had dated twenty-something-year-old men who either played their video games all day or still lived with their mamas, and she was fed up. Then, Keith had come along, 37-years-old, financially stable, physically fit, and fine as all get out, even with his sprinkle of salt and pepper hair. He was ambitious, charming, and ready to settle down again. Yes, he'd been married before, but that only added to his experience. As a hustling and bustling, 27-year-old interior designer, Alyssa had known she would marry him within minutes of meeting him. He was everything she wanted *and* needed in a man.

But his children were not what she needed right now. She laid across the bed, rubbing her temples in a circular motion in hopes of easing the incessant throbbing. She seriously needed a massage, a glass of wine, and Mario crooning in the background.

She felt her phone buzz beneath her. Rolling over, she looked down at Keith's message: *Headed home, babe. What's for dinner?* She had a good mind to tell him where he could find dinner but opted for a sweeter response instead: *Okay, my love. It's a surprise.* She threw the phone on a pillow and groaned as another streak of pain shot through her forehead. Fumbling in the nightstand drawer, she grabbed the painkillers and popped two small tablets into her mouth before laying back on the pillow and waiting for the medicine to kick in.

Minutes later, she felt her headache subside and rolled to a sitting position on the side of the bed, staring back at a picture of her and Keith on the fireplace mantel. They were leaving a football game, both of them sporting Dallas Cowboys jerseys and smiles that reached their eyes. That had been their second or third date after meeting each other at a local furniture store. Alyssa detested football, but she was willing to pretend that she was a fan if it meant that she could get closer to Keith, who was an entertainment lawyer and one of the church's most eligible bachelors. And sure enough, it worked because she was by his side for every sporting event, big court case, or gala, impeccably laced with diamonds and the finest garments.

She was the envy of many women and men. Women wanted to be her so they could hang on his arm, and the men wanted to be half the man that Keith was. And she couldn't blame them; her relationship with Keith had accelerated her career. Once an interior designer for a small company in Atlanta, she now ran her own company, selling furniture and décor with her own brand stamped on each label. She worked with some of the world's largest celebrities and elite. In sum, she was living the life she had always wanted, and being married to Keith would only sweeten the deal. The fact that they loved each other so deeply was even more than she could have asked for, and she thanked God every day for Keith.

Pounding on the door threatened to bring back her headache. "We're hungry!" The boys yelled.

"I'm coming!" She yelled back, resting her head in her hands. Standing, she looked in the large mirror leaning against the wall. Her eyes had definitely lost their sparkle a bit, and her lace wig didn't look as carefully styled as normal. The red puffiness around her eyes and nose made her usually fair skin look distressed and haggard. Turning to the side, she even noticed a slight stomach pudge, a telltale sign that she hadn't visited the gym in several days. She would be thirty-one soon, and she definitely couldn't afford to let herself go, especially if she was going to be in the public eye. Not to mention that Keith had made it relatively clear that the demise of his previous marriages happened because the women stopped caring about themselves and took their frustration out on him. She loved Keith entirely too much to lose him, so she would do all that she could to make this work.

She shook her head as the boys continued to knock and scream on the other side of the door. Yes, she would do all she could, even if it meant dealing with his worrisome children. After all, they only visited during the summer. She wiped her face, reapplied her make-up, and brushed the loose hairs back into place before plastering a smile onto her face. She needed to fix dinner.

Chapter Three

Troi

"Lord, I will liift mine eyes to the hiiills, kno—."

"No, no. Y'all stop!" Troi yelled, signaling for the musicians to stop playing, the choir members looking back at her in exhaustion. "We've been practicing this song for the last two hours, and you guys still haven't gotten that note right on 'hills.' We have to sing this song during the church anniversary program on Sunday." She made eye contact with each member, hoping they could finally get it right. She knew they were frustrated, but she was, too. She couldn't let her mother, Pastor Charlotte Moore, down again.

Everyone already knew that she was Pastor Moore's eldest daughter; they also knew that she had ran off just before leaving for college in hopes of launching her singing career. The closest she'd gotten was singing background for Johnny Gil, and now, after four years, she was back in her mother's church directing one of the best choirs in Atlanta.

She'd been surprised when her mother affectionately welcomed her back into the church and offered her the choir director position. Even though they had stayed in contact when she had run off to California years ago, she knew it had wounded her mother deeply, and it had taken even longer to repair their relationship. Once a female version of the Prodigal son, Troi could honestly say that now, she was glad to be back. Her mother and stepfather had been nothing but supportive since her return, offering her a new job and a reasonable stipend.

She loved her new position and her ability to utilize the different vocal skills and techniques she had acquired as a background singer. Even more, she loved that she had made connections in California that kept the church in the spotlight week-after-week. That's how she had met her fiancé Keshawn. He had been a musician for Kirk Franklin, who had visited her mom's church a year ago. All of the ruckus and commotion as they prepared for his performance had forced her and Keshawn together.

She had been warming up the choir for practice when her cellphone buzzed in her pocket. Looking down, she saw her Director of Music's number. Apparently, he and his wife had contracted a stomach virus and wouldn't be able to attend the concert, which meant that her choir would be without a keyboardist and drummer. Troi felt a panic attack coming on, as she gawked at his message. The choir was set to be the opening act for Kirk Franklin later that night, but they had to have music, a keyboardist at the very least. She had frantically called all the musicians she knew, but none of them could make it at such short notice.

Just when she had given up and decided on an A'capella number, she had heard the sounds of music streaming from the church's conference hall. Following the melodies, she found Kirk Franklin's crew tuning and practicing for their set. Troi sighed heavily, feeling like the clouds had opened and God had bestowed an immense amount of favor upon her.

She hurried to the big and tall man giving directions and suggestions to each member.

"Excuse me!" Troi yelled, hoping to grasp his

attention despite all the noise. She tapped him on the shoulder, causing him to turn around suddenly, a look of annoyance quickly passing over his face. Troi immediately noticed his smooth skin, a well-groomed goatee shaping his lips. She also noticed the small white spots on his face that hinted at his early-stage vitiligo, but she was taken in by the hints of gray in his eyes. She hadn't devoted very much attention to any man in a very long time, but she was fascinated by him in a way that she couldn't quite explain.

"Yeah?" He asked, rubbing his chin impatiently and looking at her from head to toe.

Troi pulled on her dreads nervously. She wished that she had taken more time to pick out her outfit today. She always managed to look like a hippy with a touch of Bohemian Chic, which is why everyone usually likened her to Lisa Bonet, but she wished she had toned it down a bit today. She was wearing brown, skinny jeans with an oversized sweater that fashioned small holes. On top of that, she sported a pair of scuffled, tan boots, her dreads piled effortlessly on top of her head.

"Hello?" He snapped his fingers in front of her face, instantly grabbing her attention. "How can I help you?"

"Oh, right, hi. I'm Troi Moore, the choir director for the Melodies from Heaven Choir." She extended her hand to him.

He took it without hesitation, his large hand enveloping hers warmly. "Nice to meet you, Troi. I'm Keshawn, the director of music for Kirk Franklin and the crew. What can I help you with?" He looked around as if waiting for something more interesting to happen.

"Oh, great! *You're* the music director!" Troi yelled with too much excitement, clutching her heart. Noticing his startled reaction, she lowered her voice. "I'm sorry. It's just that my choir is opening up for you all, and our director of music and keyboardist and his wife, who is also my drummer, is sick and won't be able to come. I really need your help. I've tried everything." She looked back at him with pleading eyes.

"Soooo, you want my crew to play for you?" There was a twinkle of amusement in his eyes. *This woman is bold*, he thought.

"Urrmm, not exactly. I wondered if I could get the keyboardist from your crew. That's all."

"I *am* the keyboardist," he drawled, leaning casually against one of the speakers and crossing his arms over his chest.

"Y-you?" She glanced at the arrangement behind him, noticing that each of the instruments were occupied except the keyboard. "I guess you are," she muttered. "So, will *you* help us?"

"I wish I could, but we still have to practice, and I don't think I can spare the time to practice with you all. I'm sorry." He shrugged his shoulders.

Troi wasn't ready to give up just yet. "Oh, come on. We're only singing two selections, and they are very simple. You'll catch on quickly without even practicing with us."

He pushed off the speakers and shook his head slowly. "I can't. Plus, I usually get paid to play."

"Oh, wow. That's what this is all about? Isn't my mom paying you all enough just to perform here?" She crossed her arms over her heaving chest, tilting her head in disbelief.

He smirked at her, seemingly amused by her comment. "First, ticket sales pay us, and just because you're mommy's little princess doesn't mean that I have to bend to your will. I'm sorry but no." He turned from her abruptly, leaving Troi stewing with anger.

She had the mind to tell him exactly what she thought about him, but as not to waste time, she marched away, hating that she ever found the man attractive in the first place. She had clearly lost her mind.

Entering the sanctuary, she relayed the news to the choir members, all of whom disliked the idea of an a'capella performance. But what other option did she have?

***

The lights burned her eyes as she whispered directions to each section of the choir, 10,000 pairs of eyes watching them now. The air was blasting, but she could feel the sweat dripping down her back. She had to pull off this performance, especially if they were going to set the scene for Kirk Franklin. She moved her fingers back and forth in front of her eyes, grasping the choir's attention as she began to count them off for the first note.

"1—2, 1—2—3—" The sound of a single note on the keyboard made her head swivel around.

Keshawn smiled and nodded at her before pressing the keys in an exaggerated display that prompted the crowd to cheer. Finally, he winked at her, giving her the signal to count the choir off again.

Troi turned back to the smiling group, a large

grin plastered across her face. The choir performed better than ever, with Keshawn catching every note and melodic shift like a professional, ushering the audience into a twenty-minute praise and worship service.

Once they had gone backstage, she waited behind the curtain for Keshawn to join them. Spotting him, she jogged up to him, enveloping him in a hug that caught them both by surprise. Not sure what had possessed her to hug him, she searched for some sort of explanation.

"Umm, th-thank-you, Keshawn. I—I mean—*we* really appreciate your help out there." She pointed towards the curtain while laughing nervously.

He seemed to be studying her, his eyes peering at her closely. "Oh, it's nothing. I wasn't sure how you'd retaliate," he teased, laughing heartily at her sour facial expression. "Plus, I couldn't possibly disappoint a woman as beautiful as you," he smiled down at her, rubbing his hand over his hairy chin.

Troi blushed under his gaze. "Um, thanks." She fiddled with her hands before deciding to just place them by her sides. "Well, I guess I should let you get to it," she clapped her hands together awkwardly before walking off quickly, refusing to look back.

"Have dinner with me!" He yelled after her suddenly, not sure why he'd waited so long to ask, especially now that he had caught everyone's attention.

Troi turned, a questionable look on her face. "Are you serious?" She whispered, walking towards him.

"As a heart attack," he whispered back, placing his hands behind his back. "Please say yes."

"Okay," she said with a slight smile. "I'll go out with you."

And she had. Now, they had been dating for a year, and just a month ago, Keshawn had proposed to an unsuspecting Troi. She had been utterly surprised because they hadn't discussed plans to be married so soon, but she loved Keshawn. Lately, she had even traveled with him, slacking on her own position as choir director just to be beside him as he ventured from place-to-place, avoiding the advances of one band groupie after another. Marrying him made logical sense, right? If she didn't, someone else certainly would.

Chapter Four

Rosalyn

City Girls' "Take Yo Man" streamed through the headphones, as Rosalyn pumped her legs on the treadmill. It had easily become her favorite song, and she was currently listening to it on repeat. *These girls know exactly how to speak to their audience*, she thought, bopping her head to the beat. They had quickly become one of her favorite girl groups, showcasing a side of life that most women wouldn't dare admit to.

Rosalyn was not ashamed of her lifestyle, it had afforded her many luxuries, even her gym was frequented by the upper echelon of Atlanta. She drove a blacked out, fresh-off-the-lot Audi, and she resided in a four-bedroom, three-bathroom home in Buckhead. And she hadn't paid for any of it. Noticing the drooling gaze of an older white gentleman, she began to run faster, her breasts threatening to pop out of her pink and black tank top. She knew it would give the old fart a rise, and sure enough, his face began to redden and perspire as he watched her. Rosalyn chuckled inwardly.

She was used to this kind of attention now, and it had served her well. Her smooth, mocha skin along with her wide hips, rounded bottom, and long legs made her an instant threat to most women. Many people would refer to her as exotic because of her Ethiopian background, which resonated in her smoldering, dark eyes and big, naturally curly hair. She had entertained a few modeling gigs here and there, but her main source of revenue was taking any woman's man, no matter his stature, race, or preference. If he had a pulse, she was confident that she could steal him and have him eating out of her hand, which meant that she didn't have to work hard for the things she wanted. She always arrived at every event alone but left with the contact information of a potential new beau. It was the easiest job a girl could ask for, but Brandon Lowe had complicated it a bit.

He was a well-known clothing designer based in

Atlanta, and he had approached her one Sunday when she was on the hunt for her next prey at the Melodies from Heaven Church of God in Christ. She had quickly dismissed him, sure that he didn't have the notoriety or cash flow to occupy another minute of her time, but then, he had made it very clear that he was only interested in her as a model for his new clothing line. She had quickly bit her tongue and taken a step back.

"Clothing Line?" she had asked, her interest immediately piqued.

"Yeah, I'm Brandon Lowe," he extended his hand. "Of Lowe and Behold Clothing."

She accepted his hand, slapping on her best smile. "Oh, I've heard a lot about you and your brand. I just hadn't seen any pictures of you before. It's nice to meet you. I'm Rosalyn." She placed extra emphasis on her name, intentionally rolling her tongue to make it sound more sensual and sexy.

He didn't seem to notice. "Nice to meet you, too. So, I'm going to give you my card." He reached into his suit pocket and pulled out a slender, gold business card. "I think you would be a great addition to my upcoming photoshoot, so if you are interested, just give me a call, and my assistant will get the information to you."

She feigned hesitance when accepting his extended card, yet another trick she had learned. She couldn't seem too eager or the man would lose interest quickly, and as far as she knew, Brandon's pockets were deep. He was probably used to women falling all over him. Finally, she spoke, "Yeah, um, thanks. I'll give it some thought."

He flashed her a boyish grin before shoving his hands in his pockets and walking away. She had called him the following Tuesday, and to her surprise, he had already found someone better suited for the centerfold; however, he thought she would be perfect as an accent model. Rosalyn had immediately felt slighted; she wasn't used to sitting on the sidelines, especially not when it came to another woman, but she was willing to play along if it meant that she had a shot at Brandon and his wallet.

When she arrived at the photo shoot location, Brandon hardly seemed to notice her. He had even insinuated that she was too stiff and needed to get in touch with her emotional side in order to properly model his garments. To say that his words had stung was an understatement. She wasn't used to criticism, but ironically, it made her want him even more.

So, she pulled from some of her childhood experiences, mustering up emotion easily. At one point, she had caught him looking at her through the camera lens, and as if in shock, he looked up from the camera and directly into her eyes. His expression immediately softened, and she found herself being photographed flash-after-flash. Before she knew it, she was being ushered into the dressing room for a different centerfold spread, and just like that, she had captured his attention and, later, his heart.

Once she'd realized that Brandon was the artsy, in-touch-with-his-emotions type, she had quickly readjusted her game plan, bringing her own emotions to the forefront and showering him with hugs and kisses that made her uncomfortable. He'd fallen quickly, offering her gifts and tokens of his affection that sent her into oblivion. He wasn't paying for her home or car, but the diamond engagement ring was enough to secure his spot on her team, and she couldn't wait until their destination wedding in four weeks.

She had even contemplated cutting off all of the other men, but one thing her mother had taught her was to: *Never put your eggs in one basket*. She couldn't afford to rely solely on Brandon out of fear that he could easily shatter the lifestyle she had become accustomed to. Nope, she would just have to be more discreet and pray to God that they made it through the one-week pre-marital counseling that Brandon had scheduled with his pastor.

Rosalyn knew that he held the utmost respect for Pastor Moore, so she already had her church smile and hug ready. *Nothing would keep her from securing the bag*, she thought, swinging her hips as she walked towards the elderly white man staring at her from the weight room.

Chapter Five

Pastor Charlotte Moore

Charlotte stared back at the photos of the four couples she would be advising over the next week. It was the first time that she would host a group therapy retreat, and unbeknownst to the participants, she was quite nervous and overwhelmed with preparation. She had conducted several pre-marital sessions, but because there were four power couples who required her attention, she knew that balancing her time would prove to be a difficult task, especially considering that she wouldn't have very much help from her secretly estranged husband, who also served as the associate pastor of Melodies from Heaven C.O.G.I.C. Also, not to mention, that her own daughter was amongst the couples. She definitely had some praying to do before next week.

Looking at the photos, she saw eight smiling faces, but she was sad to say that all of the couples didn't seem very compatible to her, like Brandon and Rosalyn. She had known Brandon before she had the mega-church and ever since he was just a pea in the pod, a playful little runt who ran around cracking jokes on Troi and swinging his little magic wand around. Even more, she knew him when he worked tirelessly to build his first clothing line, always on a rollercoaster of ups and downs and rejections, and then, his mother had died, and he had spiraled out of control for at least a year before showing back up at church for redemption. Charlotte had witnessed all of it and prayed for him without ceasing.

When he finally found his footing and established his brand, she had been his biggest fan *and* benefactor, allowing him to hold his first fashion show in the church conference hall, free of charge. She was proud for him and had confidence that he would only soar to higher heights, until she had become aware of his relationship with Rosalyn, who she knew had a knack for acquiring the interest and attention of well-to-do gentlemen.

Rosalyn wasn't a member of her church and rarely attended, except when high profile men visited. But despite her subtle warnings, Brandon had forged ahead, spoiling Rosalyn no less and eventually asking her to marry him. It had caught everyone off guard, and Charlotte felt that it was her duty to Brandon's mother to help him see Rosalyn for who she really was, using God's word of course.

The other couples were wild cards. Alyssa and Keith had recently joined the church; however, when they were in attendance, Charlotte had been told that the collection plate was much heavier. Ever since, she had been attempting to reach out to them in hopes of establishing a relationship with them built solely on The Word, not their monetary contributions.

Unfortunately, they would either leave quickly after service or find themselves surrounded by so many people that Charlotte never found an appropriate opportunity to reach out to them. However, they had attended church a few days after their engagement was announced. Charlotte was no fool; she knew that her church offered exposure for many of the elite patrons, but she finally had a reason to pull them aside. And in doing so, she invited them to the retreat, which they initially declined, but once she had let Brandon's attendance slip out, it was far too much of an opportunity for either Alyssa or Keith to pass up. They had agreed without much hesitation, the wheels turning in their minds.

Maliah and Mike, on the other hand, were different. They had both become members of the church, well before they had met at the single's mixer, and they both worked in the church, Maliah more than Mike. Charlotte couldn't say that she had been surprised by their coupling, but she *had* been shocked by their long-lasting relationship. They were both extremely headstrong, which she had learned from various times that they had attended Bible study or supervised a church project together. From the outset, they seemed to complement each other well, but she didn't know enough about them to actually oversee their wedding ceremony. She needed to see just who she would be marrying before agreeing.

And last, but certainly not least, was her dear eldest daughter, Troi. She rubbed her finger across the photo of Troi and Keshawn. She liked Keshawn, but Troi was always her wild child. When Troi had ran off to California four years ago,

Charlotte had been extremely hurt, putting her life on hold to mourn the loss of her daughter, even though she was just thousands of miles away. Charlotte had prayed more than ever, and when God allowed Troi to return home, she had rejoiced openly, offering Troi the choir director position without hesitation. Looking back now, she knew that she had done so in hopes that it would keep Troi grounded, but a part of Charlotte still feared that she would run away from her again, leaving Keshawn, too.

Keshawn was a good boy, as far as Charlotte could tell, but he was always on the road, touring with this person and that band. And lately, Troi had been on tour with him, leaving the choir to fend for itself some days. Charlotte couldn't help but worry that they both had a very delicate relationship with God, and Charlotte knew better than anyone that a marriage without God could not stand. Her own relationship with her children's father had proven that years ago, which explained why she was now on her second marriage.

Snapping out of her daze, she glanced at her watch. She had dinner reservations with James scheduled for later that evening, but there was still much more planning to do before next week. She didn't feel like sitting through another awkward meal while they pretended that their marriage wasn't suffering. Every dinner was filled with discussions about work and their weekly schedules, neither of them ever addressing the issue they had been dodging for the past several months. Picking up her phone, she scrolled through her contacts until she found James's name. She decided to text him rather than call.

Hey, honey. I'm still at the office. Can we raincheck dinner tonight? I'm swamped.

She immediately felt relieved after sending it, and she jumped when her phone chirped with a reply:

Yeah, I'll see you at the house. Be safe. Love.

And that had been it. Charlotte could feel his annoyance through the phone. But she didn't have time to focus on it. She had her sheep to look after and God's word to deliver. Her own marital problems would have to wait another week.

Chapter Six

Alyssa

"These rooms *are* kinda on the small side, babe." Alyssa twirled around slowly, scanning the room dramatically.

"Kinda?" Keith dropped his Louis Vuitton duffle bag on the hardwood floors. "I can only fit one of our bathrooms in here. Even the boys' rooms are bigger than this." He strolled over to slide open the double doors adjacent to the bedroom entrance. "This is just a closet, so I guess we're all gonna be sharing the bathroom that we passed down the hall."

He sucked his teeth, clearly annoyed. Sensing his frustration, Alyssa walked up to him and wrapped her arms about his waist, resting her chin on his back. "Think about it this way, babe. At least, we'll have direct access to Brandon. There's no way he'll say no to you." She stood on her tiptoes and placed a kiss behind his ear.

He pulled out of her reach, wiping behind his ear. "Babe!" He yelled. "You got that lipstick on. I can't have you getting it all on me." He turned to peep at his shoulder in the mirror, carefully inspecting his shirt. "Am I good?" he asked her.

Alyssa refrained from rolling her eyes. "Yeah, you're good. It's non-transferable lipstick, just the way you like it," she said dryly, lowering the handle of her suitcase and opening it to remove her clothes. She carefully placed them in one of the drawers.

While she was grateful for this opportunity to officially meet Brandon and discuss a merger between his clothing line and her interior design studio, she was secretly hoping to get closer to Keith, at least close enough to discuss their relationship and his unruly children. Peeking out the corner of her eye, she could see that he was consumed by something in his phone, which was normal, but she had hoped this week would end with him displaying more affection, outside of sex. She had already broken her own, half-hearted promise to God to remain celibate until marriage, but there was absolutely no way that Keith would agree to wait on her. What was that scripture? Something about not testing God? Well, she knew God had placed Keith in her life. Who was she to test God's decision by making him wait until marriage?

She pulled a tiny piece of material from the drawer and dangled it high above her head, loudly closing the drawer.

Keith's eyes remained fastened to the phone, as he typed incessantly.

"Babe," she drawled, dangling the red and flimsy piece of fabric in front of his face.

"Yeah?" He asked absentmindedly, never looking up.

She stepped towards him. "If you look up, you might get dessert a little early tonight."

He slowly dragged his eyes up from the phone. "Oh, yeah?" He smirked, typed a final reply, and slid the device into his back pocket. "What you plan on doing with that?" He began to walk towards her, his eyes hungry.

Alyssa gave him a devilish grin, walking backwards until her knees made contact with the rather small bed. "How about you help me out of these pants, and I'll show you," she purred, removing her shoes.

"Oh, no problem at all," he said huskily, stalking towards her. He pulled her body close against his and eased his hands under her shirt, pulling it over her head, staring back at her seductively. "I love wh—."

His phone began to vibrate loudly, causing him to immediately withdraw his hands and snatch the nagging device out of his pocket.

Alyssa sighed heavily, the fire in the pit of her stomach suddenly quenched. She scooped her shirt from the floor and tugged it over her head. Settling on the corner of the bed, she watched as Keith typed and typed on his phone. She knew not to complain because this was what she'd signed up for, and she hated how guilty she felt for wanting more from him. After all, he had given her everything. *You don't need more, Lyssa,* she thought, silently kicking herself.

Surveying the room—if one could call it a room—she noticed a large basket situated in the middle of the coffee table. It was piled high with snacks and a purple envelope. She strolled over, grabbed the envelope, and nestled her body in one of the chairs; she opened it, finding a short note from Pastor Moore inside:

Greetings, Alyssa & Keith:

I look forward to this week together, as you all prepare for your upcoming nuptials. As we venture throughout this week, I only ask for your commitment to this process, which is all about, exploring your commitment before your official declaration of rededication to each other. For that reason, you all will be sleeping in separate quarters. Please decide who will venture to the adjoining bedroom, which is divided by the large double-door closet. Also, if you look on the nightstand, you will find two questionnaires, please complete these individually. We will convene for dinner this evening at 6 p.m. in the shared dining room.

Blessings,

CM

Alyssa considered sharing the news with Keith but changed her mind upon seeing him still so preoccupied. She gathered her clothes from the drawer and dumped them messily into her suitcase before grabbing one of the questionnaires from the nightstand and approaching the adjoining bedroom door.

As the door creaked open, she glanced back at

Keith. He was oblivious to her departure. She entered the room, closed the door, and laid across the bed, her stomach growling as the fan twirled above her.

Chapter Seven

Rosalyn

Rosalyn snatched the diamond-studded sunglasses from her face, tucking them behind her ears. She frowned at the small mansion before her. It was cute, but she'd definitely seen better. Heck, she'd been gifted a much bigger place of residence from one of her many suitors.

"Wow, this is nice, right?" Brandon's voice interrupted her thoughts. He came around the car, grabbing her bag from her hands and hoisting it onto his shoulder. He looped his other arm around her waist.

Rosalyn plastered on a smile. "Baby, I was just thinking that." She swatted at his arm. "This is so ideal!" She yipped, planting a kiss on his cheek.

"Yeah, let's get inside. I can't wait to meet the other couples." He fell in stride beside her as they marched up to the door.

Rosalyn noticed the Jaguar parked next to Brandon's Porsche. It made her more comfortable knowing that at least they'd be in good company. Who knows? Maybe she'd find another piece-of-a-man to add to her list. She didn't actually need anymore; all of her bills were being covered by all of the men in her life. She mused at herself. Who else, other than her, had a man per bill?

"Babe, you okay?" Brandon asked, bumping into her as they approached the door.

Rosalyn jumped, realizing that she'd escaped to her own world for a second. "Um—yeah, sorry." She offered him a sweet smile.

He cupped her elbow softly. "Are you sure you're okay?" His forehead was wrinkled with concern.

She cupped his face affectionately. "As long as I'm with you, I'm more than fine."

He kissed her hand. "You know I love you, right?"

"Not possibly more than I love you." *And your money*, she thought, winking at him before turning to press the doorbell.

A large-framed, middle-aged white woman clad

in jeans and a floral print shirt answered the door, smiling at them warmly. "Come on in," she said, ushering them inside. "I'm Reba, the house manager for the retreat." She stepped aside so that they could escape from Georgia's Summer heat.

"Nice to meet you, Reba. I'm Brandon," he extended his hand to her. "And this is my beautiful wife-to-be, Rosalyn." He grazed Rosalyn's arm as she offered the woman the tips of her fingers.

She woman's warm smile never faltered as she accepted Rosalyn's cold handshake. "It's nice to me—."

"There's the boss of Atlanta!" A tall, muscular, and brown-skinned man yelled, turning the corner and entering the living room, making a beeline towards them.

Rosalyn's eyes fastened on his biceps, which were on full display in the tight-fitting compression shirt. She counted one, two, three—ooo, yeah—there were six abs; she had to refrain from licking her lips. Brandon looked like Comedian Lil' Rel, which made him adorable, but this man was a god. He exuded confidence and money, lots of it.

"Hi, I'm Rosalyn," she drawled, looking him squarely in his eyes. "And this," she stepped back, placing her hand on Brandon's chest, "is my fiancé

Brandon." She smiled sweetly, her eyes smoldering as the two men exchanged pleasantries. She'd hoped to capture his attention, or see some sort of attraction to her, but he hadn't torn his eyes from Brandon since she'd introduced them.

"Oh, I have heard a lot about you, man," he offered. "I think everyone in Atlanta knows who Brandon Lowe is!" He swatted him roughly on his back. "My lady loves your work. My wallet doesn't though." They both laughed loudly. "I'm Keith."

The two men shook hands again, carrying on as if they had known each other forever.

Rosalyn watched on as his pearly-white teeth sparkled in the light. She'd already peeped his Louis Vuitton sneakers and watch. She'd even seen the waistband of his Oscar de la Renta boxers. Her pulse had quickened without warning.

"And what exactly do you do, Keith?" She interrupted, interlocking arms with Brandon, who was completely oblivious to her budding interest.

"Oh, I'm an entertainment lawyer. You know, just a law man trying to make a dollar out of fifteen cents, you feel me?"

"Man, yeah." Brandon said, smoothing his beard.

Yes, very nice to meet you, Rosalyn thought, her eyes sparkling with mischief. She wasn't a fool.

Anytime a man in designer clothes and accessories played down his success, he was rolling in dough. With the right move, she would be rolling with him. If only she could find his weak spo—.

"Babe, who is it?" A petite woman asked rounding the corner.

Keith hesitantly turned to welcome the woman, cupping her elbow as she approached. "This is my fiancé Alyssa."

Rosalyn noticed that he spoke affectionately, but his eyes were fastened on Brandon. *Got it*, she thought. *Love doesn't live in their relationship. Come to think of it, love had never stopped men from pursuing her before. This will be too easy.* She pulled away from Brandon.

"Alyssa, I'm so glad that you showed up to save me from these men!" Rosalyn exclaimed. "You should've heard them carrying on as if I wasn't even standing here!" She grabbed the woman's arm and steered her towards the kitchen.

Chapter Eight

Troi

Glancing around the table, from woman to woman, the difference was astoundingly obvious. Compared to the others, she was a hippy. Troi attempted to smooth the wrinkles in her potato-sack dress, silently scrutinizing her choice of wardrobe. They were all so put together and polished. But this wasn't new. She'd always been *that* girl in the room.

"So, Troi, what do you do?" Alyssa asked, passing the basket of rolls to Brandon.

Troi formed her lips to speak. "Well, I—I," she stammered.

"We're both musicians," Keshawn interjected,

leisurely draping his arm over the back of her chair. Troi cut her eyes at him. "Actually, Keshawn is more of a musician, and I'm a singer slash choir director for the church." She grabbed the basket from Alyssa, retrieved a roll, and spread a hefty amount of butter on top of it. She noticed the look of disgust that passed over Rosalyn's face.

"Well, yeah, babe. That's what I said." Keshawn replied, straightening in his seat. "We're both in music."

"But both of us *aren't* really in music, babe." She forced a smile on her face, hoping to lighten the mood and send him a signal to back off.

"Well, they seem the same to me," Alyssa said, obviously bored with their exchange.

"Oh, well, you didn't recognize her from the Melodies of Heaven choir, so I think that pretty much shows how much *you* know," Keshawn quipped, gulping his tea as if it was the last drink on Earth.

Troi nudged him in his side, causing him to choke suddenly. She chuckled nervously while smoothing the dinner napkin in her lap. Luckily, Alyssa didn't seem bothered by his comment, and Keith looked oblivious. However, Troi noticed Rosalyn's hand steadying Brandon's leg, calming him. The menacing stare emitting from his eyes made it clear that he wouldn't spare Keshawn next time, which didn't surprise Troi. Brandon had always been relatively protective of her, standing toe-to-toe with anyone who belittled her.

She and Brandon had grown relatively close over the years; after all, for as long as she could remember, he had been a permanent fixture in her childhood home. When she'd left home, Brandon had been one of the only people with whom she'd regularly spoken. He understood her passion and never judged her. Even more, when she'd returned to Atlanta, they had continued their friendship without a glitch, well, until he had introduced her to Rosalyn. Troi had a bad feeling about her from the very beginning.

Still, Troi was embarrassed by Keshawn's behavior tonight, and she was growing tired of this side of him. He was becoming more and more abrasive with each passing day. When he wasn't cutting her with his words, he was talking over her, or excluding her. Ironically, he wanted her with him everywhere he went, but it seemed like it was only so that he could argue with her. Yes, she was tired of it *and* him.

She avoided Brandon's piercing glare. "It's

amazing that I'd never met any of you before," Troi said, changing the subject. "Well, other than Rosalyn." She cleared her throat dramatically.

"I know. I was telling Mike the same thing earlier," Maliah said, compassion twinkling in her eyes.

Out of all the women, Troi liked her the most. So far, she'd learned that both she and her fiancé Mike were educators who had met at the church's annual single's mixer. They reminded her of a young Michelle and Barack Obama and seemed to be down-to-earth and friendly in spite of all their combined accomplishments and degrees.

Keith and Alyssa, on the other hand, were an entirely different story. They had arrived at dinner decked out in name brand clothing. Keith had been talking non-stop since being seated; while, Alyssa chimed in with a retort ever so often. She looked like a Barbie doll, her make-up perfect and every strand of hair tucked in its proper place. Troi could clearly see the age difference and wondered if that factored into Alyssa's willingness to fade into the background.

"You know, I like to believe that I keep Maliah pretty calm," Mike was saying, as all of the other couples laughed.

Troi wasn't sure of the conversation beforehand, but she chuckled anyway. "I really think that all men have given themselves that title, you know, keeping us calm." She sipped from her glass of lemonade, side-eyeing Keshawn.

"Not my Brandon," Rosalyn chimed in, rubbing the back of his head. "We balance each other out." She squealed as he pulled her in for a quick kiss.

Troi swallowed hard to keep from throwing up her roll.

"I was lucky," Brandon said. "Looking at her from the outside I didn't think she'd give a brother like me the time of day, but she was so humble when I met her. She's usually the one calming me down." He cradled her hand against his cheek.

"Sounds like my Lyssa," Keith offered, caressing her thigh. The woman looked up at him with what Troi read as admiration.

"Babe, you hear that?" Keshawn asked, leaning towards her.

"Um—yeah, but you never have to calm me," Troi quipped, speaking through clenched teeth. She chuckled nervously while glancing around the table.

The other patrons shifted uncomfortably in their seats.

"Oh, you're right," Keshawn conceded. "I just try to keep her from running off on me, *too*," he snorted.

"Yo, man! That's enough!" Brandon snapped, slamming his fist on the table.

Troi blinked several times, hoping she'd heard him wrong. *Too?* She thought. Surely, he hadn't just brought up her past at a table full of strangers. She'd never left him, but it was common knowledge that she had left her mother's church to chase her dreams. She had discussed it with Keshawn; however, his decision to bring it up in mixed company was unacceptable. She was livid.

"Excuse me," she pushed away from the table, her chair loudly scraping the floor. She made it to the bathroom just as a tear slid down her cheek.

Chapter Nine

Maliah

She tapped lightly, placing her ear against the bathroom door. "Troi?" Maliah called softly. "Will you please open the door?" She heard the water turn off before the door opened partially.

Troi peeked from behind the door. "Yeah?" She sniffled, attempting to conceal her tears.

"Hi," Maliah whispered, extending a glass of water through the crack. "I just wanted to check on you."

Troi offered her a lopsided smile. "Thanks," she whispered, accepting the glass and opening the door wider. "I'm sorry. You know, it just—."

"You don't have to explain anything to me. That's not why I came. Drink some water and breathe," Maliah advised, smiling at her.

Troi obliged, then lowered the glass. "Yes, you are a *true* counselor," she chuckled.

Maliah chuckled, too. "I am, but that's not why I'm here either. I just wanted to make sure that you are okay. Wanna sit out by the pool for a minute?"

"Yeah, sure." Troi followed her through the glass doors and sat across from her in one of the wicker chairs. "You know, your past is one thing you can't run from." She sniffled, wiping her nose with a balled-up Kleenex.

"Don't I know it," Maliah sighed, crossing her legs. "Imagine not being able to run from your own past *and* someone else's," she snorted, crossing her ankles.

Troi tilted her head to the side, her interest obviously peaked. "I know we've just met, but considering what you just witnessed at that table, it's only right that you share, right?" She cracked a small smile.

Maliah folded her arms over her breasts. "That's counseling 101. You share bits of your story, and I share mine." She laughed, leaning back in her chair. "So, Mike has an ex-girlfriend who works with us. She's always buzzing around. You wouldn't believe the antics she's pulled to get him back or make me feel insecure." Frown lines accented her face.

"Make *you* feel insecure?" Troi gawked. "How? You're beautiful."

Maliah smiled, "Thanks, but I think we all have things that we aren't confident about." She shrugged her shoulders. "I didn't always see myself as attractive, especially when measured against someone like Camilla—that's her name." She leaned forward on her knees.

"Mike loves you," Troi whispered. "Anyone can see that."

"Yeah, he's great, but a man can only take so much, right?"

"Did you see Rosalyn?" Troi asked.

"Um, yeah. Why?" Maliah cocked her head to the side in confusion.

"She's supermodel gorgeous, the kind I think you're referring to, but when she walked into the room, she only had two men's attention. Brandon and Keshawn." She cackled. "My own fiancé was taken aback by her, but not Mike. He only has eyes for you."

"Wow, you know how to boost a girl's

confidence!" Maliah exclaimed. "And I'm sorry that you caught Keshawn l—."

"Girl, please!" Troi laughed. "Keshawn is many things but a cheater isn't one of 'em Plus, the girl is gorgeous. He's a man, not dead." She took a swig of her water. "I'm just sayin' that you ain't got nothing to worry about."

Maliah considered her words for a moment. True enough, Mike had never given her any reason to believe that he had been unfaithful; he put Camilla in check constantly. This was really a personal problem. She simply didn't feel that she was good enough for a man like Mike. She saw the way women looked at them when they entered social events. Every pair of eyes seemed to be asking, "What's *he* doing with *her*?" She couldn't lie; she'd been asking herself that question ever since they'd met.

"Hi, ladies," Pastor Moore sang, approaching them. "Would you like to join me and the others in the dining room?" She folded her hands sweetly in front of her torso.

Maliah looked to Troi and grabbed her hand, forcing a smile on her face. "Ready?"

The woman nodded, flashing her a warm and encouraging smile. "As ready as I'll ever be."

Maliah smiled back, hoping that she was ready herself.

Chapter Ten

Alyssa

Hmm, Alyssa thought, folding her hands under her chin. *What's going on between these two?*

Brandon sat leaning forward on the table, the muscle in his jaw flexing more and more with each passing second. Even with Rosalyn whispering in his ear, his anger remained intact as he stared Keshawn down. He looked ready to jump over the table and inflict bodily harm on him.

She leaned over to Keith, who had finally taken the time to eat. "I think I've found a way in," she whispered.

"Hmm?" He murmured, his eyebrow lifting as he cut into his steak.

Alyssa leaned closer. "With our future client."

"Oh," he whispered, his eyes twinkling with recognition. "We'll talk later."

She placed a kiss on his cheek and straightened in the chair.

"You know, my mother taught me not to whisper at the dinner table," Rosalyn drawled. "What you two love birds over there talking about?"

"Girl, nothing really," Alyssa said, waving her off. "I was telling Keith about this steak. It's delicious." She plopped a hefty fork of steak and potatoes into her mouth.

"I can't relate," Rosalyn said, feigning sadness.

"Sometimes, I hate being a vegetarian, but I can't afford any extra weight."

"Why is that?" Alyssa asked, genuinely interested in her answer.

"I'm a model," she sang, waving her hand under her face. "One pound goes directly to my chin."

"Oh, girl, I totally get that," Alyssa chimed in. "I go to the gym at least three times a week, but that's nothing in comparison to Keith." She squeezed his biceps, smiling at his knowing smirk.

"I'm a gym rat, too. I can't get Brandon to go." She playfully slapped his arm. He shrugged his shoulders, while glancing at the doorway. "Where's your membership?" Rosalyn asked, leaning forward on the table.

"I go to ABSolute, but Keith and his boys frequent Muscle Dynasty."

"*Our* boys," he corrected.

Alyssa silently chastised herself. This wasn't the first time that she'd isolated herself from Keith's children. She'd been reminding herself non-stop, but when the time came, she could never get the words out of her mouth.

"*Our* boys," she repeated, squeezing his arm.

"You all have children?" Rosalyn asked.

"I have children from my first marriage," Keith offered nonchalantly, his eyes never leaving his plate. "But since I'm marrying Lyssa, they're her sons, too."

"That's beautiful, man," Brandon said, tipping his glass of water in Keith's direction. "I can't wait to have some butt-naked kids running around. I keep telling Rosalyn to get ready because as soon as we say, 'I do,' I plan on—."

"Babe," Rosalyn interrupted, laughing nervously. "I think they know what you plan on doing." She threw her long, straightened hair over her shoulders.

"Rosalyn, do you want children?" Alyssa asked,

sensing the woman's hesitation.

"I do!" She exclaimed, clapping her hands together dramatically. "Just no time soon."

Alyssa nodded her head, but she sensed the insincerity in the woman's response. Given the meticulous nature with which Rosalyn had eaten her food, there was no way that she would allow a baby to ruin her physique. Alyssa could understand. She had her own misgivings about having children, especially since Keith had made it clear that he wanted a woman who kept herself in shape, even after childbirth. Alyssa wanted children, but not if it meant the end of her marriage.

"Yeah, man. My Lyssa here gone end up with a bunch of little rascals," Keith said. "And I don't produce nothing but boys." He shrugged his shoulders.

"Is that right?" Brandon asked.

"Yeah, man." Keith pulled his phone out of his pocket, scrolling to find a picture of he and his sons. "Here are my little men right here." He passed the phone to Brandon.

Brandon tilted the phone so that Rosalyn could see the smiling faces. "Man, they look just like you." He chuckled.

"Yeah! They're handsome!" Rosalyn squealed. "They look just like you!" A huge smile spread across her face.

Alyssa sucked her teeth, silently stewing. He was quick to correct her when it came to his sons, but he only showed pictures that excluded her. The sad part was that she'd picked out the outfits they'd worn for the photoshoot, which she hadn't been invited to. She had changed her life to be with Keith, but he had made little effort to accommodate her and her feelings. He seemed oblivious to all the exceptions she'd made just to be with him.

"Psss," Rosalyn hissed, cupping her hand over her mouth and grabbing Alyssa's attention. "I think that you and I should be friends. Clearly, our husbands are," she whispered.

Alyssa glanced at the two men, who were thoroughly engaged in a conversation about the Atlanta Falcons. "Yeah," she whispered. "I totally agree."

Chapter Eleven

Pastor Charlotte Moore

"Let me begin by welcoming each of you to the couples' premarital retreat. I pray that you have been graciously accommodated," she said, surveying the room.

Everyone nodded their agreement except for Alyssa, Keith, and Rosalyn, which didn't surprise her in the least.

"Excluding tonight, I will not attend your dinners, as we will spend a large portion of the day together," she pulled out a chair at the head of the table and sat down. "Every morning, we will meet for the group session, which will include interactive activities that will encourage you to deeply reflect on what it means to be married.

Then, I will meet with each couple; I will, also, be speaking with you individually." She smiled back at Brandon, whose eyes twinkled with anticipation, a look she knew all too well. "On Friday, the final day," she continued, "we will have the commitment ceremony, where you'll express your intentions, and that will conclude the retreat." She leaned forward with her hands planted firmly on the table. "That was just a run-down of the schedule; there are itineraries in your rooms. Any questions?"

Rosalyn raised her index finger in the air. Charlotte nodded her head, offering the woman a warm smile.

"Can we expect breakfast, lunch, and dinner from the staff here? She glanced around the room as if surveying the others. "Oh," she snapped her fingers, "and will we be able to leave the premises? I would love to do some shopping." She threw Brandon a smile over her shoulder.

Charlotte raised her eyebrows. "Ahh, those are good questions. I obviously left out some information." She rubbed her hands together. "To your latter question, you are free to do whatever you'd like, as long as you attend all required sessions. In the event that you miss a session or exercise, your time at the retreat will expire. As far as food preparation goes, for the remaining days, you all will decide which couple will prepare each meal for the day. I will provide lunch every day, so consider it team b—."

"Wait," Rosalyn interjected, "you're telling me that we signed up for a retreat, and we have to not only cook our own meals but feed everyone else as well?"

Charlotte crossed her arms over her breasts. "Exactly, Ms. Beaudreaux. I believe it will help you to see how well you can coexist with your partners, and even more how you socialize with others."

Rosalyn sighed heavily, clearly unhappy with this news.

Charlotte smirked but continued, "From what I understand Alyssa and Keith will be a blended family while Maliah and Mike are both very independent individuals who are planning to live under the same roof. Do you see?" she asked. "A simple activity like cooking together can really give you all some insight into your future lives together."

Rosalyn leaned back in her chair, sucking her teeth, her foot bouncing up and down with aggravation. Brandon patted her leg softly while giving her a reassuring grin. Her foot stilled, but

Charlotte could see the sparks flying in her eyes. "How do the rest of you feel about this?" She asked, looking about the room.

"We've cooked together from time to time," Mike offered, grabbing Maliah's hand.

Maliah nodded in agreement. "Yeah. It's been a minute, though; so, I'm looking forward to it." She squeezed his hand.

"W-we cook together a great deal," Keith stammered, moving his chair closer to Alyssa.

Charlotte noticed a look of surprise flash across Alyssa's face, which disappeared quickly and was replaced with a nonchalant smile. "That's great. Troi and Keshawn?" She looked towards her daughter.

"We on the road a lot," Keshawn murmured.

"This will be new territory for us." He grabbed his elbow, obviously bored.

"Ah, I'm glad you'll get to explore something new together. Brandon, I know how Rosalyn feels, what about you?"

He cleared his throat. "I'm ashamed to say this, but we don't really cook. I've cooked for Rosalyn four or five times in the entire year that we've been together." He leaned forward on the table.

"Man, that's pretty good if you ask me," Keith laughed, extending his fist across the table.

Brandon waved him off. "Oh, man, I wish I had more time, so I'm cool with this exercise." He rested his arm on Rosalyn's chair. "I got you, babe."

She giggled into the crook of his neck. "I know babe. I trust you."

Charlotte had to refrain from gagging. She couldn't imagine Rosalyn in the kitchen, especially in the four-inch heels that she was always wearing. So, Brandon's confession didn't surprise her. Charlotte found issues with Brandon's inability to see all the effort he'd put into the relationship. Why hadn't Rosalyn ever cooked him a meal? Either way, she knew the task would definitely expose some things for each couple.

She clapped her hands together softly. "Well, if there's nothing else, I will leave you all to make decisions about this week's menus. Please see Reba to confirm your grocery lists. And if you have any questions, you have my number. See you bright and early tomorrow for the group session after breakfast." She pushed away from the table and quickly exited the room.

"Ma!" Troi called, closing the dining room door behind her. "Hold on!"

"Hi, baby," Charlotte greeted, tucking one of Troi's loose dreads behind her ear. "What's up?"

Troi shifted her weight nervously from one foot to the other. "I was just wondering why you didn't ask me for my opinion back there?" She gestured toward the dining hall, concern lines in her forehead.

"Oh, I'm sorry, sweetie. I thought Keshawn spoke for the both of you." Extending her hand, she lifted Troi's chin and stared pointedly in her eyes. "Goodnight, my Troi." She planted a light kiss on her cheek.

Day Two

Chapter Twelve

Maliah

"They seem pretty cool if you ask me," Mike shrugged, rubbing Vaseline on his face and elbows.

"How can you say that?" Maliah frowned, shaking her head. "Keshawn is controlling, and Brandon is absolutely oblivious. I saw the way Rosalyn was salivating over Keith. And I don't even know what to say about Keith and Alyssa. They're a cute couple, but something's missing." She took the Vaseline from him and rubbed a large amount on her knees.

"Look," he said, plopping onto the bed beside her and grabbing her hand. "I'm not worried about anyone else but us. We're here for each other and that's it, so for just a week, I need you to turn off counselor mode. Can you do that for me?" He kissed her hand, looking up at her with pleading eyes.

She chuckled and squeezed his hand. "Okay, fine. Yes, I'll turn it off, but—."

He quickly silenced her with a kiss. "That's all I needed," he murmured into her lips. "Now, I'm about to kiss you until the good Lord tells me to stop."

She could feel him smiling, prompting her to grin, too. Her arms circled his neck as she leaned into him, meeting each kiss with a soft one of her own. She felt him pressing her backwards onto the bed, his hand cupping her hip. The room seemed to be spinning in a beautiful way. She didn't want it to end.

He pulled away suddenly, sarcastically gasping for air. "Woman, you're going to be the death of me." He smiled down at her, as she panted loudly.

"How so?" she asked breathlessly.

"It's hard to be this close to you and not be able to finish what I start. Normally, I can just jump in my car and go home, but you're sleeping right next door." He sighed heavily before sitting up and running his hand down his face irritably.

"I know, babe. It's hard for me, too." She sat up beside him. "I just wanna do things right."

He stood abruptly, yanking his shirt down. "Can't possibly be *that* hard for you," he mumbled.

Maliah tilted her head. "What's that supposed to mean?" She crossed her arms and glared at him.

Mike snatched his keys and wallet off the dresser. "Nothing. Are you ready?"

"I'm not going anywhere until you explain what you meant," she replied.

"It was nothing, Maliah. Let it go," he said.

"No, because this is the third time that you've made a comment like that. I've ignored it, but I think that this is the perfect time to talk."

"It's not. We gotta cook breakfast; we don't have time for this."

"Don't act like cooking breakfast is a top priority for you. What did you mean?" She pressed, standing.

"Fine! If you want me to say it, you haven't had sex before, so you don't know how hard it is to live without it! I wish you'd stopped acting like you know!" He exclaimed.

"So, you really think that living for thirty-six years without sex has been easy?!" She searched his face for understanding. His eyes quickly softening.

"I know, I know." He paced in front of her. "You already know that this is the first relationship I've been in where sex wasn't a factor. I love you, but it's hard." He sat down beside her, looking into her eyes.

"I get that. But what do you want me to do? Am I not enough until we get married? I mean, if sex was that important, Camilla has been throwing herself at you non-stop!"

He flinched and leaned away from her. "Whoa! So, I asked you to be my wife, and you're giving me a pass to go sleep with Camilla?!" He moved closer to the other side of the bed.

"No!" she yelled. "What I'm saying is that if it's so hard, why didn't you stay with her in the first place? I'm tired of being compared to her!" She quickly swiped a fallen tear from her cheek.

"I've never compared you to her, Maliah! You do that all the time, even though I've never given you any reason not to trust me." He moved towards her. "I only want you to understand where I'm coming from. Just kissing you can be hard for me. You get me excited and then, I have to calm myself down. I'm not blaming you, but I need you to know that although we committed to waiting until after the wedding, I'm still a man. I want you more than any woman I've ever met in my life." He grabbed her hand and held it in his lap, lifting her chin until her eyes were staring back into his. "I never want to make you cry. I love you too much."

She felt her resolve melt immediately as she silently chastised herself for such a rash reaction. "I love you, too. I'm sorry." She cupped his face. "I don't know. When you say certain things, I just—."

"Shhh," he said, placing a finger over her lips. "I love your mind, but sometimes, you think too much. I don't want Camilla, and I haven't wanted her since before I'd even met you. When I asked you to be my wife, I meant it. There's no other woman for me, but I can't keep having the same fight with you about her. Okay?" He asked, holding her hand against his heart.

"Okay," she conceded.

"Two years and forever to go, right?" He asked, smiling back at her.

"Two years and forever to go," she replied. "Now, let's go get breakfast started. My cinnamon apple pancakes are gonna put the other couples' breakfasts to shame!" She stood, allowing him to pull her up from the bed and into his arms.

"Wait, I thought I was making the pancakes," he stated, looking down at her. "Umm, we didn't decide last night. I just assumed since I'd mentioned it, I'd be the one to make them." He opened the bedroom door.

"No, sir," she said, walking past him and out of the bedroom. "You're not about to embarrass me."

"I make good pancakes, Liah." Mike dropped his shoulders.

"Yeah, but you take forever to cook, babe." She pulled the flour out of the cabinet. "How about you make the salmon patties?"

"Fine," he surrendered, throwing his hands up in defeat. "But I'm making the stuffed chicken tonight." He pulled the carton of eggs out of the refrigerator and sat it on the counter.

"We'll talk about it later," Maliah said, grabbing eggs and cracking them into a bowl.

Chapter Thirteen

Pastor Charlotte Moore

"Today, I'd love for us to begin by reflecting on your models of Black love. How have you seen Black love being exhibited throughout your lives?" She removed her glasses and crossed her legs at the knee. "Brandon and Rosalyn, we'll begin with you two."

Brandon leaned forward, resting his elbows atop his knees. "Well," he cleared his throat. "I haven't seen very many representations of positive Black love." He rubbed his hands together nervously. "At a very young age, my father left me and my mother. I didn't really understand it then, but I saw what effect it had on her. There were days when I'd walk in on her crying, and she'd quickly dry her face or give me something to do to keep me from seeing her." He cracked his knuckles before tugging at his knee-length shorts.

"And what do you think you learned from that experience?" Charlotte asked, jotting down notes in her notebook.

"Um, I think it taught me that love is painful, especially for women. It made me extremely sympathetic for people who want love from the wrong people and would waste away without it."

"And that's what you feel about your mother, that she wasted away?" Charlotte asked, peeking over her glasses.

"Not that she wasted away, but it seemed that after my father left, she was only living for me. She didn't have any real ambitions of her own, so in a sense, she did waste away." He dropped his head.

Charlotte watched as Rosalyn stiffened beside him. The expression on her face made it clear that she didn't know what to do with Brandon's emotions. She was clearly uncomfortable. Charlotte made additional notes, as Troi reached over Rosalyn and squeezed Brandon's hand. He responded with a stiff nod.

"And what about you, Rosalyn?" Charlotte asked, offering the woman an encouraging smile. It was the first time that she had ever seen the woman look insecure and nervous as she fidgeted with her thumbs.

"My mother and father were married and extremely happy," she stated, shifting in her seat.

"Really?" Charlotte asked, her eyebrow raised with surprise. "How long were they married?"

"For many years," she said nonchalantly.

"Wow," Alyssa murmured.

"Wow, indeed." Charlotte concurred. "And what did you learn from their marriage?"

"What do you mean?" Rosalyn asked.

"Well, I assume that you had a front row seat for the majority of their marriage. Growing up, what did you learn from your parents' relationship?"

"Um, I learned that no matter what, a husband and wife should work hard to stay together. My parents were always there for each other. They didn't even allow their children to come between them." Her eyes shifted to the floor, making it clear that she had tired of Charlotte's questioning.

Charlotte continued to take notes. "Work hard to stay together. I think that really sums up what it means to be married. I can't wait to explore that more. What about you, Alyssa?"

Alyssa shifted uncomfortably in her seat. "My

parents were like Rosalyn's—you know— together and all that good stuff."

"That's good to know," Charlotte spoke softly. "And what did their relationship tell you about Black love?"

"Umm, I guess, they showed how important it is to forgive in a relationship." She interlocked her fingers in her lap.

"Do you mind explaining how they exhibited that?" Charlotte pressed.

"Well, m—my father was an NFL player, who had more than a few indiscretions throughout the course of he and my mother's marriage, and my mom stayed through it all." She leaned closer to Keith, who squeezed her hand. "Even when my father died, and my mom found out that he had other outside children—um—she still speaks fondly of him. So, yeah, forgiveness is key I'd say."

"Okay, forgiveness. And how has that played out in your relationships?" Charlotte asked.

"I guess, it's made me more forgiving. I mean, isn't that one of the things you're always preaching about? Forgiveness?" She fidgeted nervously with the lining of her dress.

"Yes, it is." Charlotte smiled. "And Keith have you seen Alyssa modeling this forgiveness in your relationship?"

He cleared his throat, straightening his back and releasing her hand. "Yeah, I would say so—er, well—except when it comes to the boys. I don't think she's as forgiving as she can be."

"What?!" Alyssa gawked, leaning back on the sofa and putting space between them.

"Wait, hold on, Alyssa," Charlotte chided.

"You will have time to respond." She motioned towards Keith. "Please continue, Mr. Woodward."

"Like I was saying, Lyssa is the most patient woman I've ever met, especially with me. I've done a lot in this relationship, and I'm so grateful to her for being patient with me through it all. But the boys—when the boys are around, I don't really see that patience very often. She seems to always be on edge."

"That's because they break everything!" Alyssa blurted out, startling everyone in the room.

Charlotte had expected to uncover deeply buried problems in their relationship, but she hadn't expected it to happen so quickly. Quite frankly, she couldn't credit herself. It seemed that emotion was spilling out of Alyssa at a rate that surprised both she and Keith.

"They don't break *everything*," Keith said,

relaxing his posture. "You're just never prepared when they come."

"Prepared? Keith, how am I supposed to get prepared for kids who don't have any discipline?" She scoffed, turning her body to look at him full-on.

"So, now I'm a bad parent, huh? Nice, Lyss." He propped his elbow up on the arm of the sofa, starring back at her. "I guess you think that I'll be a bad husband, too. Even after all that I've done for you."

Alyssa seemed to sober immediately. "Babe, I'm not saying that you're a bad parent. You're a wonderful father, and you've been even more generous to me. I appreciate you. I—I just wish that you included me more when dealing with the boys so that we can finally get used to each other." She grabbed his hand and nestled closer to him.

Seemingly satisfied with her response, his posture relaxed, and he pulled her closer. "I hear you, and I'm going to work on that." He kissed her softly on the cheek. "See, Pastor, we know how to forgive each other and move on."

Charlotte scribbled more notes in her tablet. *That's not what I saw*, she thought. "Yes, I see," she muttered. "Let's move on." She grabbed a stack of tablets from behind her chair. "I'm going to give each one of you a notebook, and I'd like for you to write the names of at least five couples that you know personally who have exhibited true Black love. I'm not giving you a definition because I think it's different for each person, but this will help you all to see how you love and want to be loved. So, make sure that you also give me details about each couple. How do they communicate? How do they speak about each other? So on and so forth. Can we do that?" She smiled at each person, as their heads nodded. "Good. I'd like you to do this, and we will reconvene as a group after lunch to discuss. But right now, I'd like to speak with Troi and Keshawn."

Charlotte watched as the couples quietly waded out of the room. The first group session had been more in-depth than she'd wanted, which was an issue that she'd anticipated in dealing with more than one couple at a time. She definitely had to reign in their reflections to get the most out of each session.

Chapter Fourteen

Alyssa

She watched Keith from the window, as he jogged behind Brandon onto the property's basketball court. Alyssa was proud to see that all of his plans were falling right into place. Alyssa laughed inwardly. When Keith wanted something, he would stop at nothing to get it. He had pursued her the very same way.

She fondly thought of the day they'd met. She'd been an interior designer at a small company in Atlanta, and Keith had come in looking for design recommendations for one of his clients, yet another ploy to drum up new business with a high-roller. Alyssa had viewed it as an opportunity to finally launch her career. She'd worked around the clock to personally design all fourteen rooms, handpicking pieces that would accentuate the vaulted ceilings, high windows, and marble countertops. Keith had given her only three days, and he checked in at least three-times-a-day, always stressing the importance of impressing his potential client. The heat was on, but Alyssa delivered, acquiring an immense amount of gratitude from both Keith and his client.

His thankfulness came in the form of a check with more zeroes than she'd ever seen in her life and an invitation to dinner. Alyssa had agreed without even thinking, and she'd been by Keith's side ever since, becoming a major part of the package he offered to his clients in exchange for his services. He'd explained it to her as courting; he offered the client her interior design services, or season tickets, or even an unlimited supply of women in hopes that the rapper, actor, or baller would sign with him. And being the man he is, it typically worked, which meant that Alyssa was also winning.

She closed the curtains and sank into the chair nestled comfortably by the bed, sighing heavily. Keith's words during the group therapy session were still running through her mind. She'd ensured that the boys' rooms were decorated with their favorite superheroes; the freezer was fully-stocked with popsicles and ice cream sandwiches. They each had their own game consoles, comic books, and DVD collections; yet, Keith could only characterize her as impatient.

She stared down at her hand in surprise, as it gripped the arm of the chair tightly, the tension coursing through her fingers. She was angry, which was an emotion she'd worked tirelessly to deny herself. *Forgiveness,* she whispered. She exhaled slowly, her head resting on the back of the chair. If Keith couldn't see that she was really trying, she'd just have to try harder. That's one thing her mother had taught her about dealing with a man like Keith, they don't come around often, so when you get one, you have to do what you can to keep him. And by God, Alyssa was going to do whatever she could to keep hers.

She jumped from the chair, intending to go to the bathroom and freshen up when there was a soft knock on the door. She opened the door to Rosalyn of all people.

"Hey, girl," Rosalyn sang, her sultry voice taking on a rather schoolgirl tone. "I thought that maybe we could go for a run since our men have forgotten about us." She walked past her, checking out every corner of the bedroom before plopping down on Alyssa's tidy bed.

Alyssa was taken aback. She and Rosalyn had exchanged a few pleasantries but nothing that warranted a budding friendship. Nevertheless, this could be an opportunity being placed in her lap, yet another angle that she and Keith could use to get Brandon as a client. "You know what, a run sounds good! I'll probably drive myself stir crazy sitting in this house. Let me go change!"

Rosalyn beamed. "No problem! I'll wait while you change." She watched the woman hustle down the hall, closing the bathroom door behind her. "But just so you know, it's not as warm outside as yesterday!" she called.

"Okay, thanks!" Alyssa yelled back, sticking her head out the door. *Yes*, she thought. *Hooking Brandon through Rosalyn would definitely show Keith how much she wanted this and him, even his boys.* She pulled her long hair into a ponytail before flicking off the light switch and rejoining Rosalyn.

Chapter Fifteen

Troi

Troi yanked the pillow from under Keshawn's head, his smug smirk making her ten degrees madder.

"So, are we gonna talk about this session, or is getting a tan more important?"

Keshawn groaned and snatched the pillow up from the concrete. "I'll take the tan for two-hundred, Alex," he drawled.

"Well, that's too bad." Troi snatched the pillow again.

Agitated, Keshawn snatched his sunglasses from his face and sat up on the pool chair. "Look, *you* wanted to do this. Don't get mad at me for telling the truth."

"I'm sorry, and what exactly are you calling the truth?" She plopped down in a pool chair adjacent to Keshawn's staring him down. "The fact that you think I'll be a bad mother or the idea that I'm looking for a reason to leave again?"

"Both, Troi!" He yelled, jumping up, grabbing his towel, and marching towards the house.

"No! No! You don't get to run out," Troi yelled, blocking his entrance. She could see the frustration bubbling in his eyes, but she didn't care. He'd embarrassed her, and it didn't help that he'd said everything in front of her mom, the one person who suffered the most from her first sudden departure.

"Troi, get out of my way!" Keshawn yelled back, attempting to push past her.

Troi stood firm, placing both arms on his biceps. "No! We came here to fix whatever it is that's making you so angry! Keshawn, I—I just don't understand. I've turned down several choir workshops and singing opportunities just to show you that I'm in this. I'm in this for you. I want *you*. What more do you want me to do?!" She could hear the desperation in her voice, and she couldn't say that she liked it. The last time she'd heard herself this worked up, she'd gotten into a heated argument with her mom about following her dreams of being a singer. The next day, she'd caught a flight. She placed her hand over her chest, hoping to ease the pressure she felt mounting up and threatening to halt her breathing.

Keshawn's defenses seemed to falter a bit, but anger continued to flash in his eyes. "Troi, you hate hearing the truth. The truth is that you're spoiled. You think that the world revolves around you. Always reminding me about your potential contracts and offer letters. I'm not trying to marry you to become your background singer! Your mama might run her house and husband like that, but that ain't what I'm signing up for!"

Troi flinched, "Leave my mama out of this! You don't have the right to comment on my mom or her marriage. What's wrong with you?!"

"Look, look, look," Keshawn cooed, grabbing her hands. "I'm sorry. I didn't mean that. I'm just stressed with the wedding, these tour dates coming up, and now this retreat." He ran his hand across his face. "I don't mean to take it out on you. Will you look at me?" He bent down, forcing her eyes to meet his.

Troi assessed him from head-to-toe, her resolve

softening. "Keshawn, I'm not trying to overshadow you. If anything, the Bible tells us that a woman should be a man's helpmate. That's what I've been trying to be. I sit in on most of your sessions, offer suggestions, and even synchronize all of your calendars. I'm trying to help. That's all."

He dropped her hands suddenly. "Did I ask you to do any of that? And how long before you get tired of pretending that being with me is enough? You're the daughter of the great Pastor Charlotte Moore. I watch people's eyes brighten up when you walk into the room. Even worse, half of 'em don't even seem the least bit interested in me until you walk in. So, you keep *trying*, but frankly, I'm tired of being in your shadow and waiting for the other shoe to drop." He flung the towel over his shoulder. "And, no, I don't think you'll be a good mother or even a good wife. You'll always be searching for more than I can give." He stepped around her and stalked back to the house.

Troi stood stunned, watching him walk away as if he hadn't just slapped her multiple times. She stared into the pool, the warm Georgia breeze sending ripples through the clear blue water. She knew she should feel some kind of emotion right now, but all she felt was an urgent need to dip her feet into the inviting water. She reached down to remove her sandals before sitting down, swinging her legs over the side of the pool, and hissing as the coolness engulfed her feet. She exhaled slowly before leaning back on her hands, her eyes tightly shut.

"How's the water?" a deep voice asked, interrupting her thoughts.

Troi jumped, shielding her eyes to see beyond the shadow towering above her. "It's really cool," she murmured.

"Mind if I join you?" Mike asked, already removing his loafers.

"No, help yourself," Troi drawled, unable to tell him that she really needed time to be alone.

"Thanks," he said, lowering his body to the concrete. "Whew! That's cold!" He yelled, his face scrunched up in disfigurement.

Troi couldn't contain the boisterous laugh that tumbled from the pits of her stomach. "Oh, my God. You should see your face!" She doubled over again.

Mike chuckled. "That bad, huh?"

"Worse!" She yelled. "I needed that," she sighed, sobering.

"Glad I could help," he offered. "I think we all

need a laugh." He rubbed his hands together, his friendly eyes meeting Troi's.

"Oh, not you and Maliah. You guys are so good together. I wish I could say the same for me and Keshawn. I just don't know."

"Well, isn't that why you're here? To sort it all out, right?" His feet moved back and forth slowly under the water.

"Yeah, but it seems like it's getting worse," she shrugged. "We're just in limbo."

"Well, that's one thing Maliah is always saying. Sometimes, it has to get worse before it gets better," he bumped his shoulder against hers. "Wow, don't tell her I just said that." He rubbed his hand over his forehead.

Troi chuckled, "No promises. I think this would really make her day."

"Yeah, and I'll never hear the end of it," he chuckled. "Man, that woman drives me crazy, but I'm just as crazy about her," he whispered.

Troi knew it was her turn to bump his shoulder. "I think that a person would have to be blind not to see that. I wish we were all that blessed."

"I'm not worried about everyone else seeing it. I need her to see it," he sighed. He looked over at her, noticing the solemn expression on her face.

"Hey, you'll get there. It just takes time. Trust me."
He enveloped her hand in his and cast her a
reassuring smile.

"What's going on?" Maliah asked, marching
towards them, both Troi and Mike turned towards
her, surprise etched across their faces.

Chapter Sixteen

Maliah

"So, what? You were just being Mr. Comforter, huh?" Maliah hissed, throwing him yet another disgusted look as she placed the last pan in the dishwasher.

Mike slowly raked his hand over his face. "You tryna be funny. But yes, Liah, that's all." He placed the tub of leftovers in the refrigerator before turning back to her, leaning against the countertop, and crossing his arms over his chest.

"You're engaged, Mike!" she said through clenched teeth. "Your own fiancé needed comforting, but you're out at the pool all cozied up with some other woman, who is also engaged—and let's also add that she happens to be the pastor's daughter!" She slammed a forlorn cup on the counter.

Mike raised both hands. "You really need to calm down. I'm pretty sure that this isn't in the counselor handbook—"

"Don't bring my job into this!" She lamented. "The point is that you left me in here to finish cooking dinner so that you could go comfort someone else. See! That's our problem. You're Mr. Charisma when it comes to everyone else, but as soon as we disagree, you walk away from me every single time!" She slammed the refrigerator door.

Mike pushed away from the counter. "No! You create problems! We're in here cooking, having a good time, but then, you start complaining that I'm not doing this or that right. Next thing you know, you're bringing up past women I've dated and asking how I cooked with them. It's almost like you can't stand to be happy and drama free. As soon as we fall into a groove, you drum up something to fight about. I don't know if it's your insecurities or what, but I can't keep doing this with you, Maliah! It's gettin' real tired." He turned to leave the kitchen.

"See," Maliah chuckled. "There you go leaving again. Bet you wouldn't do that with Camilla and now Troi."

He turned back towards her. "No, I probably wouldn't," he spat. "They probably wouldn't be as insecure as you."

Maliah recoiled, his words immediately silencing her. She watched helplessly as he stalked from the room, tension evident in his hunching shoulders and balled up fists. He was angrier than she had ever seen him, and she couldn't understand why. Surely, he knew that holding another woman's hand was unacceptable, and if he didn't know, what else was he capable of doing behind her back. She'd never snooped through his phone or even went through his wallet, but now, she was wishing that she had.

It wasn't that he had ever given her any reason to doubt him. It was just—Camilla—Troi—they both fit the profile of women he'd dated before her: short, petite, mellow, and self-assured. Even though they had totally different styles, it was that flippant disregard for other people's opinions that resonated from them. Mike possessed that same tenacity, and more than anything, she kept asking herself, *Why me?*

"Maliah, can we talk?" Troi whispered, entering the room quietly.

Maliah's eyes flashed with anger. "No." She brushed past her. She turned abruptly, "We may not be friends, but I didn't think I had to watch out for the pastor's daughter, too. Now, I see why Keshawn is so controlling. You can't control yourself." She stared her down before turning and marching out of the room, leaving Troi's mouth hanging wide open.

Chapter Seventeen

Rosalyn

Their run had been a total bust. Alyssa had spent most of the time asking about Keshawn and his business while ducking and dodging all of Rosalyn's questions about Keith. On top of that, the girl was flat-out irritating. All that smiling and giddiness made Rosalyn sick to her stomach. Now, Rosalyn knew how to play the dumb chick, too, but this girl was stuck on stupid for real. It's like she couldn't see her life beyond Keith. Everything was *me and Keith this* or *me and Keith that*, which let Rosalyn know that he must be a backbreaker or laced with dough. Both options were enticing, but Rosalyn knew better than to let a man have her whipped. Nope! Wasn't happening, not now or in the future. She'd been there, done that a long, long time ago. It had nearly ruined her life, much like it was killing this poor girl Alyssa. She just yapped and yapped.

Rosalyn rubbed her temples with both hands, hoping to ease the nagging voice that accompanied her mere thoughts of the girl. She'd been sitting on the edge of the bed stewing ever since they'd returned. Luckily, Brandon was still out playing basketball, which meant that she had time to take a bubble bath while checking in with her pro-baller boo, Cedric.

See, he was a point guard, or center forward for the Atlanta Hawks, and they'd recently made the play-offs, which meant that she had more time to play around with Brandon while Cedric attended mandatory practices. He was one of her star players, so she had to make time for him, even if it meant a little dirty talk in the tub.

She yanked her shirt over her head, twisting and turning in the mirror. *Yeah, girl. You still got it,* she thought. Her phone began to buzz on the dresser. She walked over, inhaled sharply as she recognized the number, and flipped the phone on its face. Like her friend De'Leon used to say, *Ain't no point in dragging the past into the now. Not today. And definitely not tomorrow.* As soon as the phone stopped buzzing, she scooped it up and began dialing.

"Hey, baby. You got time for me?" She cooed, chuckling inwardly when Cedric's breathing steadied, a clear sign that he had dropped the weights he'd been lifting. *Exactly how I like 'em*, she gloated while turning on the hot water.

Day Three

Chapter Eighteen

Rosalyn

"Baby, you think you can flip these pancakes for me?" Brandon asked, running to the trashcan to dump a bowl full of eggshells.

Rosalyn lowered the magazine to the countertop and slowly climbed off the barstool. First, he'd asked her to help him with the pancake mix measurements, and now, he couldn't even flip the pancakes by himself.

She strolled over to the stove and grabbed the spatula. She flipped each pancake and shot Brandon a glance. "Umm, babe. The pancakes are burnt," she said dryly. "You burnt them." She flattened the pancakes more and grabbed the mixing bowl.

Brandon walked over to her, grabbing her waist. "Dang, baby. It's probably the second time in my life that I've ever even made pancakes," he laughed.

"So, what are we gonna do? We can't serve these burnt pancakes to everyone?" She asked, a bit more annoyed than she intended.

"Um, can you mix a new bowl of pancake batter?" He checked his watch. "I mean, we only have thirty minutes before everyone comes down for breakfast." He dumped a handful of shredded cheese into the bowl of egg yolks.

Rosalyn's nose twisted up in agitation. "I mean, I can, but you know I don't really like cooking." She plastered on a smile and placed a slow, sultry kiss on Brandon's neck.

Rather than bend to her will, he stepped backwards. "Well, babe. I get that, but the whole point is for us to work together, which, also, means that we can learn together. So, come on. We got people to feed. Grab that bowl." He slapped her hip playfully and attempted to kiss her cheek.

Rosalyn side-stepped him and dumped the charcoaled pancakes into the garbage can. "But baby," she wined. "You aren't marrying me because I can cook. You already know that's not something

I enjoy. Can't you handle this one by yourself?" She flashed him a large pair of puppy-dog eyes.

He seemed to be falling for it, but then, he dumped the eggs into the pan and grabbed a spatula. "Like, I said Rosalyn. I need you to at least try." He stirred the eggs back and forth in the pan. "Make some toast or something," he commanded absentmindedly.

She scoffed at him, her mouth hanging open. Since she'd met Brandon, he had never spoken to her with such authority, which was what she liked about him, at least in comparison with the other men she entertained. While the others flaunted their money around, commanding and dominating everyone around them, Brandon was much more giving and sentimental. He rarely told her no and would literally drop everything when it came to her. But now, she was afraid that this stupid retreat was changing him, and she couldn't have that.

She grabbed the loaf of bread from the cupboard and pulled out several slices. "How about you make omelets and bacon for everyone, and I'll do my best to fry some bacon and make toasts?" She bumped her hip against his.

He leaned backwards to kiss her cheek. "That's my girl."

No, I'm not, she thought. No matter how hard he tried, he definitely wasn't going to turn her into some 'wait-by-the-door' homemaker. In her life, she'd done everything she could to keep from being that kind of woman. It didn't suit women well. Just look at the other women in this house; all of them tripping and looking stupid over a little bit of testosterone. She flipped her hair over her shoulders, as she turned back to the stove.

I would much rather be at the nail salon right now, she thought.

Chapter Nineteen

Pastor Charlotte Moore

Talk about pulling teeth, Charlotte thought, scribbling notes on her pad. Today's group therapy had been tense, well mainly between the women. Each of them seemed relatively tight-lipped, which had only caught Charlotte off-guard when it came to Maliah and Troi. Something had happened, and Charlotte would definitely need to speak to the house manager to find out.

She stuck the pen behind her ear and linked her fingers together in front of her torso. "Well, I think it might be a bit more beneficial if I speak to some of you individually. I'd like to begin with Alyssa." She smiled at the woman, who seemed the least bit interested in speaking to her. "So, you all can exit now; Keith, please stay on stand-by because you're next." She looked on as the couples filed out of the room in silence.

When the door closed, she turned to face Alyssa. "So, I'd first like to say thank you for staying so that we can talk." Her smile was met with a stiff nod. "I'd like to start by asking if there's anything that you'd like to say before we begin?" She placed her glasses on top of her head.

Fidgeting with her fingers, Alyssa straightened up on the sofa. "Um—well—I think that Keith and I are stronger now than we have been in a while." She plastered on a fake smile.

Charlotte thoughtfully placed her index finger under her chin. "After just one day?"

Alyssa crossed her legs at the knee and rested her hand on top. "Well, yes. I really think that yesterday's session helped me to understand the role that Keith and I play in each other's life. I think that it can be easy to forget that sometimes."

"And what role would that be?" Charlotte asked, picking up her notebook and repositioning her glasses on the tip of her nose.

"Well, the Bible says that I am his helpmate, and I believe that I bring that to our relationship. At the same time, he is my tree, keeping me grounded and protecting me. Through it all, we have each other's best interest at heart, I believe."

"Those are powerful words, Ms. Lawrence. Very powerful," she murmured as she scribbled. "You always do a really great job of helping me segue into my next points. I'd like to play a word game of sorts with you today." She pulled a stack of flashcards from the back panel of her notebook. Is that okay?" She peeked over her glasses, while placing ten cards face down on the table.

Alyssa shrugged her shoulders and moved to the edge of the sofa. "Sure. I like games."

"I'm glad to hear that. I'd like for you to flip the cards over and move them around until they spell a word. You do not have to use every letter for the first word that you choose to spell out. Do you understand the game?"

The woman nodded her head, clearly anxious to begin. She turned over the letter *U*; then, *I*. Next, there came *S-M-S-V-B-S-E-*and *I*. She tilted her head in confusion before commencing to eagerly move the letters around on the table.

Charlotte made a note of this almost antsy behavior. It seemed that Alyssa relished in being given a task, so much so that her eyes hadn't left the table.

"Okay, there's the first word." She knocked on the table. "M-I-S-S, Miss," she said, looking up at Charlotte.

"Good, that gives us a great place to start." Charlotte closed her notebook and leaned forward, touching each of the four letters. "The term *Miss* has typically been reserved for unmarried women under thirty. In this case, we're going to use it in reference to a much younger *Miss* Alyssa. Can you tell me a little about the teenage you?"

The woman sat back on the sofa. "Yeah, well, I'm not sure that there's much to tell. I was a scrawny, lanky teenager with bushy eyebrows and knobby knees," she chuckled, her eyes rolling towards the ceiling. "I could've been the poster child for every movie about being bullied."

"And were you bullied as a teenager?" Charlotte asked softly.

"No, not really. I mean, my dad was the great Ezekiel Lawrence, one of the highest scoring shooting guards in the NBA. If anything, I had more trouble weeding out fake friends than getting them. We were all ugly teenagers trying to find our way." She rested her elbow on the arm of the chair, a clear sign that she was becoming more comfortable.

"But you *did* find your way. How did you change from being that ugly teenager to the beautiful young woman before me today?" Charlotte pried.

"My mom," Alyssa looked down at her dress with a warm smile. "It happened out of the blue really. One day, my mom came home with an enormous bag of make-up, hair extensions, and clothes— there were so many clothes—clothes that were different from her normal style. I walked into my parent's bedroom, and she was trying on this hideous wig, twisting and turning in the mirror, and when she saw me, she snatched it off and told me to come sit at her vanity. She pulled out this stack of magazines from one of the shopping bags and told me to find a girl that I thought was pretty. I chose this girl similar to me, brown and tall. I showed the picture to mama, and she said, 'Okay, well, let's turn you into her,' and that was the first make-up lesson that I received. Mom wore make-up but not like the women in the magazines." She rocked back and forth on the sofa, smiling fondly.

"It was like I became her doll. She plucked my eyebrows, straightened my natural hair before applying the longest hair extensions I'd ever seen, lined my lips, and even allowed me to put on one of her new dresses, which had to be cinched at the waist with a belt. At the end, I slipped on a pair of heels and twirled around and around in the mirror. Mom went on and on about how pretty I looked, and that my first experience with make-up." She cleared her throat, seemingly snapping out of her reverie. "That is one moment I remember as a teenager."

"Wow," Charlotte said. "That must have been a major moment in your life for you to remember it so vividly."

"I mean, yeah, because mom had never come home like that before. It was as if she was on a mission to re-invent herself or try something new. I don't know, but I guess it sticks with me because of how it made me feel."

"And how did it make you feel?" Charlotte asked.

"Pretty, I guess. For the first time, I felt pretty and girly. I'd been a tomboy up until that moment. Don't get me wrong, I was still boyish afterwards, but I think that moment caused me to gradually shift to a more feminine side."

"Well, I can definitely see that being the case," Charlotte said, chuckling and motioning towards Alyssa's fit and flare, pink dress and floral-print heels."

Alyssa glanced down and laughed, too, lifting the corners of the dress from the sofa.

"But I'd like to revisit something you said about your mom." Charlotte began to read from her notebook. "You said that she seemed to be on a mission or wanted to reinvent herself that day. What did you mean? Or what gave you that impression?"

"Well, you'd have to know my mom. She's the epitome of class, never a strand out of place. Her closet was filled with pale blues and nude colored suits and heels. I mean, she had been an accountant before marrying my father, so I guess you can say that she was very calculated with her attire. She was a lady, but on that day, she came in with these loud pinks, reds, and orange colors; heels that were more than three inches high, and weave. My mother always wore her hair in a bun or chignon at the nape of her neck; even though she had beautiful, wavy tresses, she only let it down at home. But all of her old clothes went out, and the new clothes came in. Not to mention, she began to experiment with make-up that she didn't even need. Sometimes, I think she got so frustrated with it all that I'd see her crying while sitting at her vanity. So, I learned and helped her wherever I could." Her voice trailed off, as she wiped a fallen tear from her chin, refusing to look at Charlotte eye-to-eye.

Charlotte extended a box of Kleenex to her. "That was very nice of you. You must really love your mother, not all teenage girls would be that concerned," she said softly.

Alyssa shrugged, dabbing at her eyes. "Well, for most of the year, it was just me and her. Daddy was always traveling for games and stuff, so it was always mommy and me time at my house."

"That's sweet, and what about your father? How did he react to seeing your mom all dolled up?" Charlotte asked, watching the woman closely.

A cloud seemed to suddenly sour Alyssa's rather soft expression. "He—he didn't really fawn over her the way I thought he would, but that was dad. He wasn't the very expressive type. He told her she looked pretty and then asked about dinner."

Charlotte scribbled some more. "Okay, I think this a good time to make a new word with the cards. This time I'd like for you to use all of them. I'll give you a hint. The full word begins with an *S*."

Once again, Alyssa quickly busied herself with moving the cards around, chiding and talking to herself throughout the process. Finally, she set back and stared down at the letters before looking up at Charlotte. "Submissive?" She frowned.

"Now, what does that word mean to you?" Charlotte asked.

"It means being willing to give in or be obedient," Alyssa offered, biting her nails.

"Okay and in your opinion, what does that word mean in a marriage?"

"Well, I think it means the same. Someone giving in to his or her spouse."

"Did you see this word in play in your parent's marriage?"

"Yes, at times."

"Who was being submissive?" Charlotte asked.

"Mostly, my mom, but I think she liked for my dad to be in charge. They had an understanding that he paid all the bills and gave her shopping or just-because money, and she handled all of the household duties. But when he needed her to make a good impression on sponsors at award shows or benefit dinners, she was always right by his side."

"But other than financially, did your father ever have to show up for your mom, I mean—for anything unrelated to him, you, or basketball?"

Alyssa glanced at the ceiling thoughtfully before taking a deep breath and averting her eyes back down to her folded hands. "Um, when you put it that way, I guess the answer is no. Me and my father's needs were her main focus." She fidgeted with her hands before finally dragging her teary eyes up to meet Charlotte's.

Chapter Twenty

Troi

She tapped on the door, pressing her ear up against the heavy wood. It swung open suddenly, causing Troi to stumble into her mother.

"Oh, hi, mom," she murmured, attempting to regain her composure. "I wasn't sure if you were still here."

Her mother pulled her glasses from her face and perched them on top of her head. "I decided to take a bit more time in the office to go over my notes from today. But I'm glad you stopped by. Give me mama a hug." She extended her arms.

Troi seemed to fall into her mother's arms, squeezing her tightly before hesitantly releasing her.

"That was some kind of hug," her mother said, looking back at her with genuine concern. "Is everything alright?" She was still holding Troi's hands.

Troi eased her hands to her side and followed closely behind her mother, sitting adjacent to her large desk. "Well, I guess, everything is as good as it can be considering the circumstances." She shrugged her shoulders nonchalantly.

"Okay, you're gonna have to tell me. Did you come here to speak to your mother or your pastor? I'm trying to set boundaries where I can." Her mother swiveled from side-to-side in her chair.

"I know, I know. I asked for those boundaries. I think I need to speak to my mom right now, I guess."

"Okay," her mother came around the desk and sat in the cushioned chair beside Troi. "So, what's wrong?"

Troi exhaled slowly. "I just need to know how you and James work through things like what me and Keshawn are dealing with right now? Like, I know your position as pastor strained your marriage with Dad, but how have you and James made it work?"

Her mother cleared her throat. "Well, let me say that being a pastor can be difficult. The whole idea of balancing my personal and spiritual life sometimes takes a toll. With your father, yes, I was still building the church, but I think that some resentment settled in once he realized that my dream was taking off much quicker than his. And I don't mean to put your father down; I loved him. But I think that's the major difference between him and James. James is more supportive and understanding, maybe *too* understanding at times." She shifted uncomfortably in her seat. "Don't think that the work you and Keshawn are doing right now means that something is necessarily wrong. Marriage means being willing to do the work over and over again and trusting God in every situation. As long as you have God and the right partner by your side, it's all worth it."

"And me and Keshawn. Do you think we're right for each other?" Troi waited patiently while biting her bottom lip.

Her mother leaned forward and grabbed her hand. "One thing I learned when you left and went to California is that Troi Marie Moore has her own mind, and she must feel in charge of her own flights, failures included. So, I can't tell you what you need to figure out for yourself." She smiled and rubbed Troi's cheek. "Now, I've been meaning to talk to you about Vacation Bible School. I'd like for you to oversee it this year because mama needs a vacation."

Troi smiled inwardly. She didn't necessarily desire children of her own, but she thoroughly enjoyed interacting with the kids at church. She'd discussed several ideas for kid-level entrepreneurship and music programs with Brandon, who had readily agreed to assist her, so this would be the perfect opportunity to meld their interests together while, also, teaching them about God's endless love.

"Sure, mom. I'd love to help. You and James deserve a vacation."

"Yes. Yes, we do," her mother agreed, squeezing her hand.

Chapter Twenty-One

Maliah

"She has serious trust issues," Mike said, crossing his legs at the knee. "It's like no matter what I do, she's going to find something wrong."

Maliah remained quiet, with her arms crossed tightly. She hadn't spoken to him since yesterday, despite his efforts to communicate with her from time-to-time.

Charlotte looked to Maliah, making a mental note of her standoffish body language. "Maliah, are you feeling up to this today? If not, I can just speak with Keith," she offered.

Maliah straightened in her seat. "No, I'm fine."

"But are you *really* fine?" Charlotte pressed. "Your body language is telling me that you're not.

Can one of you tell me what recently transpired between you?" She looked back and forward between the two.

Maliah and Mike exchanged glances, neither of them wanting to delve into this subject, especially considering that it involved the Pastor's daughter.

Mike cleared his throat and shifted in his seat. "Okay, let me first say that all of this happened because Maliah jumped to conclusions without giving me the benefit of the doubt. First, we argued over how to best prepare chicken parmesan. If something isn't completed the way that Maliah envisions it, she just shuts down. It's like she can't maneuver around anyone else, but she expects everyone to conform to her. And Pastor, that's not how this marriage thing is supposed to work." He slouched back onto the chair, clearly frustrated.

Charlotte leaned back in her chair. "Well, you're actually very much correct in that regard. Marriage is about compromise. And that can be very difficult. Maliah, would you say that Mike's assessment of the situation is correct?"

Maliah unfolded her arms and exhaled slowly. "I'm a counselor, so I'm used to having the answers for people. I know that I envision things in my head and when executed differently, it can sometimes throw me off kilter. So, he's right. That's something I can definitely work on. However, I'm here. I stay to do the work. Mike, on the other hand, walks at the first sight of trouble. He did the very same thing yesterday, and then, I found him holding another woman's hand. So, now I'm like, if it's that easy for him to leave me but console someone else in distress, what will he do once we're married?" She looked at him expectantly.

Charlotte cleared her throat. "It's a lot to unpack in all of that. Let's first start with the most troubling part. Mike, would you like to explain the handholding that Maliah witnessed?"

He shifted uncomfortably in his seat. "I would. I would have been even more happy to explain it yesterday, if she'd given me the *benefit of the doubt*. Yesterday, I'd just argued with Maliah over dinner, and Troi had just had a disagreement with Keshawn. So, instinctively, I tried to reassure her that everything would be okay. It wasn't romantic at all. I'm a school principal, so I'm used to doing this all the time. I pride myself on being caring and attentive to other people's needs. Sometimes, it's hard for me to break out of that mode, but I meant no disrespect."

Charlotte sat her tablet on the coffee table between them. "Well, I think that's what Maliah is getting at. You had an argument and left the room. And what we know is that distance doesn't do much to improve a relationship or communication. So, you can see why she felt slighted seeing you consoling someone else and not her, right?"

He lowered his eyes to the floor and nodded his head slowly. "Yeah, I can." He turned to Maliah and grabbed her hand. "Look, I'm sorry. I never mean to put anyone other than God before you. I love you. I never want you to feel as though you are in this relationship alone, and I now understand that when I walk away that's how it makes you feel. I'm sorry for that."

Maliah wiped a fallen tear from her cheek. "I know it was innocent, and I know that I have to work on my own issues. I'm sorry, too, and I love you."

He reached over and wiped the hanging tear before gently kissing her hand. "Clearly, we both have things to work on." He looked at Charlotte. "Pastor?"

Charlotte smiled. "I think admitting that work needs to be done is the first step, and you both just completed it. I commend you on being so open and transparent. The love is so clearly there between you two, so now, we need to advance your trust and communication. What I see is that Maliah has a real need for reassurance which was more than likely caused by a breach of trust in her past; while, you, Mike struggle with communication in uncomfortable environments. And both of you are used to being in control, which is a hurdle that I expected from the very beginning," she chuckled. "So, I'm going to give you a few activities that I would like for you to complete tonight. If done correctly, they will explore avenues of trust, control, and communication. Is that okay?" Both nodded. "Good. So, you'll do these tonight, and I'll check in with you tomorrow. Good job today." She handed Mike a folder.

They both stood, said their goodbyes, and walked hand-in-hand out of the room.

"You know, I hate it when we're not talking," Mike said, closing the door and turning towards her.

"Me, too," she said.

He pulled her closer, until their bodies seemed to be melting into each other. "And I'm absolutely pissed off that it's been hours since I've kissed you. We can't keep doing this, Maliah."

Maliah rested her hands on his shoulder, looking up into his pained face. "I know. But you don't have to wait anymore." She reached up and pulled his lips down to hers, igniting a fiery kiss that she didn't know she'd been waiting for. All her resolve turned into mush while enveloped in his strong hold.

The sound of someone clearing her throat pulled them apart.

Maliah turned to find Pastor Moore looking on with laughter tugging at the corner of her lips. "Sorry, Pastor," she chuckled, wiping her mouth with her hands.

"Remember separate rooms!" The pastor called after them, shaking her head, as she ventured to her car.

Chapter Twenty-Two

Alyssa

She pulled the warm clothes out of the dryer, dropping a pair of Keith's boxers on the floor. Scooping them up, she scowled and stuffed them into the basket. Hoisting it in the crook of her arm, she swung open the laundry room door, nearly running into Keshwan, who was also holding a large basket of clothes.

"Whoa, there!" He chuckled, reaching out to steady her.

Repositioning the clothes on her hip, she tucked a lose strand of hair behind her ear. "Sorry, I didn't know that anyone else was in the house," she chuckled nervously.

"Yeah, the other ladies already left. You chose laundry over shopping?" He sat the basket down on the floor.

"Well, someone's gotta do it right? You know how y'all clothes begin to smell after a game of basketball, right?" She shifted the basket to her other arm, more than ready to end this awkward exchange.

Keshawn nodded. "Yeah, I know how that is. You know, I wish there were more women like you. Maybe I wouldn't have to do my own laundry," he scoffed, kicking the basket.

Alyssa stared down at her feet uncomfortably. It was one thing to have cordial banter, but it was another thing to blatantly compare your fiancé to another woman. She didn't know why he had such a chip on his shoulder. Considering what she knew about them, Troi seemed fairly chill to her.

"Well," Alyssa said. "Every woman's different. Troi's great."

"Y—yeah, she is," Keshawn agreed half-heartedly, picking up the basket swiftly.

"I—I'll see you later," Alyssa said.

"Yeah, see y—Wait." Keshawn sat his basket back on the floor again. "Let me help you with that." He reached for the basket in her arms.

"Oh, no. You d—". She wasn't able to finish before Keshawn effortlessly grabbed the basket from her arms. "Well, thank you. Our room is just down the hall." She led him to the room, where he sat the basket beside the bed.

"It's really nice and tidy in here." He glanced about the room, surveying every corner. "You don't even want to see my room." He placed his hands on both hips.

Alyssa offered a slight smile before dumping the clothes on the bed. "It's just how I like things. I'm not completely OCD, or anything. I just prefer order is all."

"Yeah, I see." His gaze fell upon her, causing her to shift her weight from one foot to the other, as she folded a pair of Keith's gym shorts. "Well, let me go. I know the guys are probably waiting for me at the court." He nodded his head and exited quickly.

That was weird, Alyssa thought, shaking her head. *I don't understand why he seems so unhappy with Troi. She's a melting pot of boho chic and warmth, if you ask me.* She stuffed a pile of Keith's clothes in the dresser drawer.

***

"So, what did you say to that Pastor Moore?" Keith asked, flopping down at the end of her bed and removing his sneakers.

"What do you mean?" She asked, closing her laptop and pulling her hair back into a ponytail.

He turned towards her, his eyes piercing into hers. "So, you're really going to act like you don't know what you said?"

Alyssa raised her hands in confusion. "I mean, I won't know if you don't tell me, Keith. I'm not a mind-reader," she drawled, re-opening her laptop and avoiding eye contact with him.

He came around the bed and set directly beside her, closing the laptop and tilting her chin upwards. "Don't forget why we're here," he chided. "There is nothing wrong with us. Brandon Lowe. That's the goal of the week." He kissed her forehead and stalked through the adjoining room's door.

Alyssa exhaled slowly and removed the laptop from her lap, folding her hands behind her head and leaning against the headboard. She didn't know what it was, but all of a sudden, trapping Brandon didn't seem as appealing to her now. She loved Keith, and she was willing to do all that she could to support him. However, she wasn't sure that what they were doing was right anymore. In fact, she was becoming unsure of a lot lately.

"Hey," he peeked into the room. "I'm about to jump in the shower. Join me, if you want." He winked at her before closing the door.

Alyssa folded her arms and chewed on her bottom lip. She stole several glances at the door before pushing her laptop to the side and throwing the blanket from her legs. She may not be as sure about Keith's dealings with Brandon, but one thing she knew for sure was that he never disappointed her in one area.

Chapter Twenty-Three

Troi

"Okay, what else do you desire in a future wife?" Troi asked between clenched teeth while eying Keshawn.

He continued to slouch in his chair. "I'd like for her to be supportive." He crossed his arms tightly.

"Good," Charlotte said. "I'm glad that each of you took the time to complete the activity I assigned to you because now we have some things to start today's session. Your expectations." She smiled while looking from one somber person to the other.

"Troi, how do you align with Keshawn's outlined expectations?" She removed her glasses and looked to her daughter.

"I don't," Troi scoffed, raising both hands in resignation. "I'm supportive and extremely affectionate, but his expectation of a domestic wife just isn't me."

"Well, let me stop you there," Charlotte interrupted. "We don't really know what facets of domesticity he desires. So, you can't say what you aren't if you don't know how he defines it." She turned towards Keshawn. "Do you mind telling Troi what you mean by domestic?" she asked him, peering back at him expectantly.

He sat up in his chair. "I mean it in the most traditional way. I'd like a woman who doesn't mind settling down and making a home with me, which means allowing me to take care of her and our future children," he shrugged nonchalantly.

Charlotte jotted down a few notes in her tablet before turning to Troi. "Okay, now tell Keshawn how you feel about his expectations."

Troi smoothed the wrinkles in her linen dress and cleared her throat. "Well, I don't think your expectations are unrealistic. I'm extremely supportive, even so far as to put many of my responsibilities on the backburner to assist you. However, I dislike it. I enjoy working for the church and traveling for various workshops and trainings but knowing that I have my church family waiting for me when I return." She smiled, glancing at Charlotte. "So, while I'm willing to compromise in some ways, I don't want my life entirely wrapped up in my husband. I need something for myself. And children aren't on my radar right now." She exhaled slowly while peering into Keshawn's eyes.

Charlotte leaned forward with her elbows resting on her knees. "Now, Keshawn, I don't want you to respond. I'd like for Troi to explain her expectations, and likewise, I'll give you an opportunity to respond."

Troi inhaled deeply. "I, like Keshawn, want someone who is supportive, but I think that most important is for me to marry someone who is genuine."

"And what do you mean by that?" Charlotte asked, taking notes.

"I mean someone who genuinely loves God because then he'll know how to love me."

Charlotte turned to Keshawn. "And how do you align with that?"

He shrugged, offering a long sigh. "I mean, I love God. I'm the minister of music. I don't understand." He sat forward, his eyebrows raised with aggravation

Charlotte calmly touched his hand. "Wait, don't get worked up. Troi's expectations aren't an attack on you but, rather, what she desires. Okay?"

He offered her a stiff nod and crossed his legs at the knee, his eyes drilling a hole into Troi.

"Now, I think it's important for both of you to understand that no one is perfect. We all have a list of expectations that our spouses do not completely check-off. What you have to decide on prior to getting married is what expectations you must have without a doubt. So, what boxes are you unwilling to accept being unmarked. Hmm?" She looked between them before clapping her hands. "Okay, so here is a list of general expectations. Tonight, I'd like for you both to check all that you'd like in a spouse; then, on the front of this miniature post-it, write those that are your must-haves." She handed both to them and removed her glasses from the tip of her nose.

Troi and Keshawn exchanged glances before filing out of the room.

"You think we can spend some time together tonight?" Troi asked, turning to face him.

He rubbed his hand roughly over his hair. "Can't. I gotta send my group this music tonight."

He stuffed both hands in his pocket and rocked back and forth on his heels. "Sorry, babe." He reached for her elbow.

Troi stepped out of his reach and waved off his hand. "No. We're supposed to be here working on us, not your music." She crossed her arms over her chest and lifted her chin, clearly agitated.

"I get that, but I still got bills to pay, Troi," he said, his head tilted to one side.

"Fine," she sighed, turning to leave.

"No, Troi. Wait." He grabbed her arm, attempting to pull her towards him.

"No!" She yanked her arm out of his hand and glared up at him. "Go work, Keshawn."

He looked back at her in confusion, which quickly faded and morphed into blatant frustration. He threw his hands up as if to protest but shrugged in defeat, before stuffing his hands back into his pockets and walking in the opposite direction.

Troi stared after him with her mouth hanging open, as she fought back the tears that threatened to spill from her eyes.

"Yo, Troi. What's going on?" Brandon asked, rounding the corner and removing his headphones. He placed his hand on her arm, concern reflected in his eyes.

Troi looked up at him in silence before laying her head on his shoulder and releasing a myriad of emotions, as he enveloped her in a strong embrace. They stayed that way for longer than she expected, but Brandon didn't seem to mind. She pulled out of his arms, wiping her tear-stained face.

"Sorry," she sniffled. "I guess I didn't know how much I needed that until now." She attempted to smile, which came out like more of a lopsided grin.

Brandon nodded sympathetically before gently wiping her face with the sleeve of his sweatshirt. "How about we go for a ride?" He tilted her chin upward and offered a reassuring smile.

Troi chuckled. "Ok—"

"Babe?" Rosalyn interrupted, glancing from one person to the other before decidedly dismissing Troi. "You think we can go to the mall?" She rested her hand on his arms while pressing her breasts against him.

Brandon put space between them. "Sure," he said, glancing towards Troi. "But it'll have to wait until tomorrow. I gotta run an errand with Troi real quick." He kissed her on the cheek and grabbed Troi's hand. "Let's go."

Troi tried to hide her surprise as she ran to keep

up with his long stride. She looked back to find Rosalyn still standing in the middle of the hall, her fists balled up by her side.

Chapter Twenty-Four

Rosalyn

Who does he think he is? Rosalyn stewed, slamming her bedroom door. *I don't even have to be here. And then ditching me for Troi, of all people.* She paced back and forth in front of the bedroom window.

Sudden movement on the basketball court stopped her. It was Keith coming in from his evening run.

Well, she thought. *I guess there's a silver lining in everything.* She dashed to the bathroom, squirted a hefty amount of oil in her hands, and rubbed it on her shoulders and down her cleavage before readjusting her dress so that her best assets were in plain view. *Alright, girls. Let's work.* She winked in the mirror and strolled out of the room.

She found Keith huffing and puffing near the kitchen entrance. "Hey," she greeted, feigning surprise. "How's the heat out there?"

Keith slapped his hands together and rubbed them down his shirt. "Uh, it's not too bad actually." He stretched his arms behind his back while allowing her to pass by him.

"D—do you wanna join me?" Rosalyn asked, fidgeting with her hands. *I'm a pro, and he doesn't even know.*

He looked towards the stairs. "I—I should be getting up to —"

Rosalyn cupped her hand over her mouth. "I'm sorry. I wasn't even thinking. I guess I just thought we could talk about you possibly representing Brandon. He could really use a new lawyer." She waved him off, just as his sparkling eyes became trained on her. "But nevermind, I understand if you have to get to—"

"No," he said, rubbing his chin. "I'd be glad to join you." He reached around her and opened the door, waving his hand for her to exit first.

Rosalyn flipped her hair over her shoulder, as she stepped onto the concrete leading to the pool. One thing she knew about men like Keith was that if they wanted something, there was absolutely nothing they wouldn't d o to get it. At first she'd thought he was gay seeing how he pined after Brandon, but the more she talked to the dodo bird Alyssa and watched them when Brandon was around, she knew it was strictly business. After all, she couldn't blame Keith; he'd obtained her respect. He was looking to secure the bag, and she was all for it. *Hmph, we could do it together*, she thought, sashaying seductively towards the pool, as he followed closely behind her.

"You know, it's hard to believe that Brandon doesn't already have a lawyer. His work is everywhere." He scrunched up his gym shorts and settled onto the lounger.

She crossed her legs, the slit in the dress revealing her perfectly toned thighs, immediately catching his attention. She watched as he ran his tongue across his lips before dragging his eyes back up to her face. *Ah and you're a cheater, too*, she thought.

She chuckled, grazing his arm with her hand. "You've been around Brandon. He likes to do things for himself; he doesn't really want people to see him as part of Atlanta's upper echelon. You know how that goes," she sucked her teeth.

Keith looked puzzled. "I don't get that. He *is* the upper echelon. It's only going to become more and more dangerous for him, if he doesn't have the proper representation."

Rosalyn could tell that he was trying extremely hard to keep his eyes fastened on hers. "Well, now that's where I can help you." She ran her finger down his arm slowly. "I'm going to be his wife in four weeks. So, I don't mind pushing him in your direction."

Keith's eyes followed her finger, which was slowly traveling up his arm. He chuckled, "I'd like that, but I'm guessing that's not all you want." He leaned towards her, her body growing warmer under his hot stare.

She licked her teeth before swinging her legs to the side of the chair. "That's absolutely not *all* that I want. Think you can help me with that?"

He looked back towards the house before turning back to face her. "Without a doubt." He grabbed her hand and pulled her into the poolhouse, unaware of Maliah and Mike, who had both just returned from a picnic.

Chapter Twenty-Five

Maliah

"I really think we should say something," she whispered, tying the scarf around her hair.

Mike plopped down beside her on the bed. "Liah, I don't think that's a good idea," he said, shaking his hand.

"Wouldn't you want to know?" she asked, turning towards him suddenly.

"I—I mean, yeah," he stuttered. "But these aren't our friends. We just met these people. How do we know they'll even believe us?" He slid closer to her, grabbing her hand and massaging it gently.

"I-I just—No, stop that!" She groaned, trying to pull her hand away from him. "You're trying to distract me."

"Oh, yeah?" he asked, placing a soft kiss on the inside of her palm. "Is it working?" He looked at her through downcast eyes.

"Yes," she giggled, slapping at him playfully. "But, babe, I'm for real. Alyssa and Brandon need to know. I haven't had the opportunity to really speak with Alyssa, but Brandon is very nice. Honestly, I think he'd be better off with Troi, but that's just me." She sighed heavily before turning to Mike, frown lines pulling at the corners of her lips.

Mike dropped her hand. "Okay, what is it?" He moaned.

"Oh, nothing. But I just want to be sure that this is what you want. Marriage is very important to me, Mike. It's a commitment, and I know other people might not take it serious, but I do."

He was silent for a moment and then, grabbed her hand. "Maliah Rose Jamerson, you are the only woman for me, that includes yesterday, today, and forever more. I have never been a cheater, and not because I couldn't but because I am a man after God's own heart. I know I love you because I love Him, and I can vow to you that before I hurt you, I will walk out of your life." He grabbed her other hand. "Woman, trust me when I say that I'm not looking for any reason to lose you." He leaned forward until his forehead was touching hers. "I love you, Maliah," he whispered.

Maliah cupped his check. The stubble pricked her fingers softly, but she loved it. "I love you," she whispered, allowing his lips to meet hers. "And if you ever cheat on me, I'm going to cut you where the sun don't shine." She poked his chest.

He laughed loudly. "Understood, counselor. Now, tell me you love me again." He kissed her on the lips.

"I love you," she whispered.

He kissed her again. "Say it again." He pulled her onto his lap.

She released a squeal, always enjoying his ability to simply pick her up as if she didn't weigh over two hundred pounds. She laid against him, confident that he could handle her and at the same time hold her heart. Without a doubt, Mike was the man God had ordained for her, and she wanted to spend the rest of her life proving it to him. Everyone wasn't so blessed.

***

She'd tossed and turned for the past hour, unable to catch an ounce of sleep. She swung her legs over the bed and stuffed her feet into her slippers before making her way to the kitchen for a glass of water.

"Can't sleep either, huh?" Troi asked, startling her.

Maliah walked towards her with her hand over her pounding heart. She'd heard voices coming from Troi and Keshawn's suite and assumed that they were talking, so seeing Troi sitting on one of the kitchen barstools had caught her by surprise. "Girl, no," she said, shaking her head and reaching into the cupboard. "I've just been lying awake in bed for the past hour." She ran some water from the faucet into the glass and joined Troi at the counter.

"Yeah, me too. Keshawn's in his room working on a new piece, and I've just been up, mind running all over the place." Troi tapped her fingernails nervously on the countertop.

"Wanna talk about it?" Maliah asked, nudging her. "I mean, I am a counselor." They both laughed.

"Yeah, but I don't think even you can fix this," Troi murmured. "You know, some things just aren't worth fixing I don't think."

Maliah sipped on the water. "I totally get that. I used to date this guy in college who was just so opposite of me. He smoked, drank, partied, and kissed everyone's butt, but I stayed with him for over two years, just fighting to be with him. All for it to blow up in my face. I thought staying meant that I was fixing things or working on us, but when you're the only one working, it becomes a form of abuse. So, trust me, I get it." She squeezed the woman's hand.

"This man," she spoke softly. "Keshawn is not the man I met years ago, Maliah. I don't know this man anymore."

"Well, let me ask you this. Are you the same Troi he met years ago?"

Troi looked to the ceiling thoughtfully before smiling and shaking her head. "Not at all."

Maliah emptied the glass. "Welp. There you have it."

Troi chuckled. "You know, you're pretty good at this counseling thing. Too good. You should probably bill me at this point."

Maliah laughed. "You sound like Mike." She nudged her with her elbow.

"I'm glad we're cool after that whole pool thing," Troi said. "If nothing else comes from this week, I would at least like to leave knowing I have a new friend." She offered Maliah a hopeful smile, one that she knew was genuine.

"Girl, don't even mention it. I'm sorry for even acting like that. I knew there was nothing going on when I saw it, and I would like for use to be friends." She smiled back.

Troi jumped from the barstool. "Well, I guess I'm gonna try to get some sleep. We have one more full day to get through, ain't no telling what might happen next." She slouched towards the bedroom.

"Alright, good n—Troi!" Maliah called, standing up.

"Yeah?" Troi asked, turning towards her, dark circles forming under her eyes.

"I have something that I need to tell you," Maliah said, shifting her weight nervously from one leg to the other. *This is not our business, Liah.* Mike's words were running through her mind. "Try not to think about tomorrow but about what you love the most. You'll go right to sleep," she said, plastering on a cheerful smile.

"Hmm, I'll try that. Thanks. Have a good night," Troi said while yawning and strolling back to her bedroom.

"Night," Maliah murmured, placing the glass in the sink. *Hopefully, one of them would get some rest.*

Day Four

Chapter Twenty-Six

Alyssa

Keith hadn't spoken to her since he'd returned from his run last night, even though she'd tried numerous times to spark up a conversation. He'd simply mumbled his replies and left as quickly as he could. So, she hadn't been surprised when he refused to assist her with breakfast this morning. Instead, she'd rolled out of bed, pulled her hair into a ponytail, and stared in the mirror for longer than she'd expected, ultimately deciding not to wear any make-up.

She opened the cupboards looking for the vanilla extract, which she knew would definitely enhance her French toasts. Finding it, she did a little dance before measuring a teaspoon and pouring it in the egg batter.

"Good morning," Troi said in a singsong voice, opening the refrigerator and grabbing a bottle of orange juice.

"Good morning," Alyssa replied, a bit more enthusiastic than she expected. "How'd you sleep?" She stirred the batter slowly.

Troi hopped up on the barstool. "Not bad actually. Maliah gave me some really good advice last night."

Alyssa's eyebrow raised. "Oh, yeah? What was that?" She asked, genuinely interested in Troi's answer.

Troi took a swig from the bottle. "She basically told me not to think about any problems but instead, think about something that I love. So, I thought about singing and the workshops I lead, and I was out like a lamp." She snapped her fingers and smiled.

"Wow. I might need to tr—"

"Hmph. Can't believe it wasn't me that you thought about," Keshawn interjected, opening up a cupboard and grabbing a coffee cup. "Good morning, Alyssa." He lifted the coffee pot and poured a hefty amount, ignoring Troi, who rolled her eyes.

Thank God I overprepared, Alyssa thought, taking a sip of her own coffee. "Good morning, Keshawn."

"You need help in here?" he asked, settling on one of the barstools.

Alyssa watched as Troi spit a mouthful of orange juice back into the bottle, surprise and disgust on her face.

"You're unbelievable," Troi hissed, jumping from the chair and marching out of the room.

Keshawn waved her off and turned to face Alyssa. "Where's Keith?" he asked, looking towards the door.

Alyssa readjusted the oven temperature before placing a pan of diced potatoes inside. "Well, he's still in bed. Had a long night."

"Didn't we all?" He said sarcastically, running his fingers through his tiny curls. "But I was serious, if you need help, let me know."

"I don't think that will be necessary, but thanks for asking," she said, refusing to make eye contact.

"You know, I think Keith is crazy. I'd be sitting on cloud nine if I had a woman devoted to me like you are to him. Selflessness is a virtue I find extremely attractive in a woman," he said, sipping his coffee, his eyes raking her body from head to toe.

Alyssa fidgeted nervously with the bread she'd just pulled out of the bag. *Surely this man isn't flirting with me while his fiancé is mere steps down the hall. What a scumbag!* She thought.

Instead, she smiled and placed a few slices of egg-coated bread in the pan. They began to sizzle immediately, mimicking exactly how she felt right now, trapped and looking for a way out. She could easily tell him where to put his compliments, but she'd always played the role of peacemaker. Even when it came to her mother and father, it had always seemed that she was the only thing keeping them together, which Pastor Moore had brought to her attention at yesterday's session.

Even worse, she was beginning to realize that Keith's ambition and business ventures were the only thing holding them together. After all, he'd been unfaithful to her more than once, and being the peacemaker that she was, she'd cried and hurled insults at him, only to take them back later, going back to business as usual.

She flipped the French toasts before turning to face Keshawn, ready to tell him just what she thought about him. "I-I-I should go check on Keith," she said, silently chiding her cowardness. "Can you watch these for me?" She pointed to the pan.

"Sure," Keshawn drawled, climbing from the stool and purposefully brushing past her. "By the way, you're even more beautiful natural." He winked at her before removing one slice of bread from the pan.

"Uh, be right back," Alyssa murmured, quickly walking to her bedroom, even more thankful that she wouldn't have to prepare dinner tonight.

Chapter Twenty-Seven

Troi

She was over it. She didn't need Keshawn to do any more to prove how much they didn't need to be together. The little tactic he'd just pulled with Alyssa was the nail in the coffin, as far as she was concerned.

She paced back and forth in her room, while talking to God. "God, I haven't done everything right, and oftentimes, I disappoint you. I'm so sorry. I don't want anything or anyone that you haven't ordained for me. God, if it isn't your will, please remove it all from me right now. Please God." Tears ran down her face as she fell backward on the bed, already knowing the answer to her prayer.

A soft tap on the door, elicited a groan from her lips. She really hoped it wasn't Keshawn trying to apologize, but she doubted it would be. She snatched open the door, finding Brandon on the other side.

His smile quickly faded into concern. "What's wrong, Troi? What he do?" He asked, scanning the room behind her.

Troi chuckled. "Nothing that he hasn't already done, but these tears weren't for him. Wanna come in?"

He seemed to relax a bit. "Sure." He strolled past her, as she stepped aside. "So, why were you crying?" He sat on the chaise at the foot of her bed.

Troi slid next to him, wiping her face. "I guess I finally accepted the fact that God didn't ordain my relationship with Keshawn. All of this was our doing, and nothing will go right if we fail to consult God, first. That's what happened when I ran off to California at eighteen, and that's exactly what's going on with me and Keshawn right now. So, these aren't sad tears. I'm disappointed in myself, Brandon."

Brandon slid closer to her and tilted her chin with his finger. "I get that," he said. "But the Troi

I've known for most of my life has not been a disappointment. The decisions you made were ones that you needed to make to get to this point right here. Isn't that what 2 Corinthians 12:9 tells us? At your weakest, you are yet strong. That's how I see you right now, Troi. The strongest woman I've seen in a very long time." He moved his hand upward until it was cupping her face.

Troi slid her hand over his, smiling up at him. "Thanks, Brandon. You always know what to say."

He smiled back at her before blinking several times and clearing his throat, suddenly removing his hand. "Um, I should probably get to the therapy session with Rosalyn," he said, standing and walking towards the door.

"Hey, Brandon?" Troi called standing, as he paused with his hand on the doorknob. "We both know that my relationship is over, but I wouldn't be a real friend if I didn't ask you about Rosalyn. Did God ordain your relationship?"

Brandon appeared stunned, looking back at her with a blank expression. "I gotta go, Troi," he said, rushing out of the door and closing the door behind him.

Troi exhaled slowly. She'd unknowingly been holding her breath since he'd entered her room, which was an unusual reaction to Brandon. They'd practically grown up together, but after hanging out with him last night, discussing frivolous things, eating too much ice cream, and laughing about all the stupid stuff they'd said as kids, she'd been more inclined to see Brandon as more than that chubby little boy that followed her around everywhere as kids; he had become an upstanding man, one that was far too good for Rosalyn. She just hoped he would figure it out before it was too late.

Chapter Twenty-Eight

Rosalyn

Her tongue passed slowly over her lips, as she repositioned the slit of her floor-length dress.

"Rosalyn?" Pastor Moore called, leaning forward in her chair. "Did you hear what Brandon said?" She looked at Rosalyn over her outdated glasses.

Rosalyn repositioned her body on the loveseat and cleared her throat. "I'm sorry, baby." She rubbed Brandon's hand gently. "I must've zoned out for a minute." *Because this is not how I would be spending my time, if it were up to me,* she thought.

Brandon removed his hand from out of her reach. "I think that's part of the problem, Rosalyn," he drawled. "If it's not what you want, you're not interested."

"That's just not true," she whined. "I go to all of your little fashion shows and preview thingys all the time," she waved her hand dramatically.

"Little?" Brandon sneered. "Now, I really see how you feel, huh?"

She attempted to grab his hand again. "Oh, no, baby," she pouted, blinking her eyes dramatically. "You know that's not what I meant. I'm just saying that fashion is your passion, not mine. However, I'm willing to go because I want to support you, and I love you." *And the accolades don't hurt*, she thought.

"I mean is that really why you go, Ros?" He tilted his head to the side and stared at her straight on. "Look me in my eyes and tell me that's really why you go," he said, his eyes never leaving hers.

Easy peasy, she thought, facing him and grabbing both of his hands. "Brandon, baby, I go because I love you, and I want nothing more than to support you." She flashed him her biggest smile, which must've worked because she could see his shoulders begin to slump again.

He kissed both of her hands. "Well, I'm glad to hear that. I just don't want to get in a marriage that isn't built on real love," he said. "I've seen how that goes," he murmured.

"And how does that go?" Pastor Moore asked, crossing her legs.

"Not good," he replied. "My mother was in that kind of relationship with my father for years, and it only broke her down."

"And how does that play out in your relationship with Rosalyn?" Charlotte prodded, much to Rosalyn's dismay.

Brandon looked over at her. "I just don't want a relationship where both people aren't pulling their weight, emotionally and financially."

Rosalyn's head popped up instantly. "What do you mean by *financially?*" she asked, her voice growing. "We agreed that I would stay at home, maybe have a few children, and see to your paperwork and stuff."

"Y-yeah, I know, but I'm not sure that's the best plan for our relationship anymore. That's one thing that this retreat has definitely helped me realize."

Rosalyn's leg bounced nervously, as she folded her arms over her chest. "Don't you think that's something you should've spoken to me about before making a decision?" She sucked her teeth, anger building with every passing second.

"I mean, babe, that's what I'm doing now. Talking to you about it," he said.

"No, if we're supposed to be a team, you should've brought this up to me *before* we got in here," she hissed. *Especially not in front of this little preacher*, she thought.

"I think that Rosalyn has a point, Brandon. This is definitely something you should have spoken to her about prior to this session. Your failure to do so may suggest that you don't see her as an equal partner in your relationship."

Rosalyn leaned back on the sofa, giving the pastor a once over. *My girl, you may be smarter than I thought.* She redirected her attention to Brandon. "I would agree with her assessment."

Brandon cleared his throat. "I mean, we aren't on the same playing field financially or emotionally. I give more in both situations. I believe in taking care of my future wife," he said, waving towards Rosalyn. "But I would also like for her to have something of her own and be there for me emotionally."

"But that wasn't our agreement," Rosalyn said through clenched teeth.

He flinched as if burned. "Don't make it sound like a business arrangement, Rosalyn. That's part of the problem," he chuckled, shaking his head.

"Let me interject here," Pastor Moore chimed in.

"Marriage in many ways is like a business arrangement. You both are supposed to present your demands and then, decide what you will or will not agree to. What I'm hearing is that Brandon's terms have changed, and Rosalyn both wasn't aware and does not agree with them. Is that a correct assessment?"

Rosalyn and Brandon exchanged glances. "Yes," they both replied.

"And that is a problem that cannot be swept under the rug. You want to begin your marriage on harmonious terms. Tomorrow you all will participate in a commitment ceremony. In preparation for tomorrow, I'd like for the both of you to fill-in these marriage contracts." She handed them both a cardstock piece of paper with multiple lines for their terms of agreement. "Please complete these separately and thoughtfully and bring them to the ceremony tomorrow. Tomorrow you will decide whether or not you can agree to your partner's terms. Understood?"

"Yeah, sure," Rosalyn drawled, stuffing the paper in her purse. *The sooner we get out of here, the better.*

Chapter Twenty-Nine

Pastor Charlotte Moore

This week had already been more than she'd expected, not only for the couples but for her personally. To see Troi and Brandon grappling with each of their relationships had really bothered her. And with the final day quickly approaching, she wasn't sure how it would end. She hadn't considered that all of this could backfire on her, with each person leaving the retreat without having grown at all. The last thing she wanted was to negatively impact their relationships with each other and possibly God.

She lowered her head in prayer:

God,

Please continue to give me the words to say to your people. Correct me when I'm wrong and lead me in the right direction when I attempt to veer off course. May you get the glory in all of this. And God, if you will, please help me fix my own marriage.

Amen.

She grabbed each couple's portfolio, which had been filled with her notes and their assignments from the week. With the exception of Rosalyn and Brandon, each of the couples had successfully completed their tasks, which had resulted in powerful conversations that she knew they wouldn't have faced without her nudging.

Take Maliah and Mike, for instance, they seemed to be overcoming a major hurdle, which was Maliah's trust issues, but the jury was still out; Mike seemed to have reached his breaking point this week. She wasn't sure how Maliah's need to be reassured would pan out for him.

Similarly, she could tell that Troi was looking for a reason to trust that her relationship with Keshawn was, in fact, God's plan. All of their assignments had encouraged some deep reflection for each of them. Keshawn's assignments were only partially complete; while, Troi had carefully answered each question. Charlotte knew her child, so it was evident to her that Troi wasn't saying half of the things that she felt. However, the boundaries Charlotte had set for herself restricted her from prying too deeply into Troi's personal life. She had to trust that she could make the best decisions for herself.

Alyssa and Keith, on the other hand, seemed set on being together. In the sessions, she'd seen lightbulbs come on in Alyssa, but the following day, it was as if Keith had pressed the reset button, and Alyssa was right back where she'd started. She hadn't had very many opportunities to learn about Keith's previous infidelities, but she wasn't sure that anything would come of it anyhow. Like Keshawn, Keith had also half-answered the assignment questions, or hardly participated in many of the sessions. And as of late, he seemed to be even more withdrawn and distracted, giving Alyssa little to no support or response in their sessions. So, she hadn't been surprised to learn that Alyssa had cooked breakfast by herself this morning; in all honesty, she'd expected it, which was the primary reason that she'd only assigned them one meal this week.

Lastly, Rosalyn and Brandon seemed to be on the cusp of a major transition, but she wasn't exactly sure where it was going. Someone would have to compromise, and Charlotte couldn't see that happening with either person. Charlotte knew Brandon; when his mind was set on something, nothing could budge it. However, right now, his mind seemed set on Rosalyn, while hers was trained on his wallet. *Surely, Brandon can only be oblivious for so long*, Charlotte thought, shaking her head, her glasses hanging from her lips as she looked over their assignments. Like Keith and Keshawn, Rosalyn hadn't answered many of the questions.

Charlotte closed the last folder and slouched in her chair, sitting her glasses on top of her head. The couples definitely had some major decisions to make before they were ready to walk down the aisle. She glanced at her watch; she had her own marriage to work on.

Chapter Thirty

Alyssa

She had heard enough. Snatching her toiletries from the dresser, she stormed out of the bedroom to put as much distance between them as possible for fear that she might say something she would later regret, truly crushing his pride.

And yet again, she thought rolling her eyes, *here I am taking his feelings into consideration even though he said everything he could to hurt me.* She chewed on her bottom lip anxiously, her mind reeling. He had spoken with such contempt and disdain that she felt like a piece of her had fallen off a shelf and broken into several pieces, and no matter how much she mulled over it, she couldn't quite pinpoint the moment that he had started feeling this way. She'd made a valiant effort to be the kind of woman he said he needed, supporting him to no end. All she knew at this exact moment was that today's activity had clearly awakened some resting demons in her husband-to-be, and she intended to get to the bottom of it if their future marriage would have a fighting chance.

"God, please, help us," she whispered, fumbling with the towel wrapped loosely around her petite frame. Tiptoeing to the community restroom, she hoped that the others hadn't heard them arguing. Compared to relationship, the other couples seemed to be extremely ready for marriage. She couldn't confidently say that she was anymore, if she ever could. But she wanted to think that the foundation of her relationship could outlast any dilemma or disagreement that came their way. After all, they had been together for years, staying together through far worse; surely, one week couldn't ruin everything she had worked for.

She turned the shower knob to the far left, satisfied by the steam that began to rise, letting her know that it was perfect. After undressing, she slid behind the shower curtain and proceeded to wash her hair; the water passed softly through each strand and cascaded down her back. She envisioned her man's hands gliding down her stomach and resting on her hips. She knew that the mere thought was a sin and that the act itself would violate the promise she'd made to Pastor Moore, but what else was she supposed to do right now? It felt like forever since he had touched her affectionately, and she needed reassurance that he still wanted her.

Or else— She shook her head vigorously, hoping to clear the doubt that never failed to rear its ugly head. No matter how hard she tried, it was always lurking in the distance, just waiting for an opportunity to destroy all confidence she had in herself and her relationship. *He loves me; I know he does*, she thought, running the soapy towel over her shoulders.

Just then, she heard the shower door slide open behind her. She wanted to leap into his arms because this would be a first. Even though they had verbally agreed to avoid sex during the retreat after nearly getting caught last time, the old adage "desperate times call for desperate measures," seemed to be at play, and she couldn't be happier that for once *he* had taken the initiative and joined her. Not to mention that he wasn't the type of man you told no, and she was desperate for reassurance.

With her eyes closed, she relished in his touch as his arm snaked around her petite form while his hand roamed through her hair.

"Nice of you to join me," she whispered. Her body melted against him as she cupped his face, her eyes flying open in alarm. She turned quickly, wiping soap suds from her eyes. Her mouth fell open at the sight of Keshawn, naked and smiling down at her.

"This was what you wanted, right?" He smirked, attempting to push her wet hair behind her ear.

"No!" Alyssa exclaimed, knocking his hand from her face and scurrying out of the shower. She quickly wrapped the towel around her body. "What do you think you're doing?!" she yelled.

He turned off the water. "I mean, what you expect? I've been flirting with you all week, and you weren't objecting!"

The door swung open as Keith burst into the bathroom. "What's going on here?!" He asked, coming into the room. "You're sleeping with my fiancé?!" Keith exclaimed, lunging towards Keshawn, who had tied the shower curtain around the lower half of his body.

"No, Keith!" Alyssa yelled. "H-h-he—"

"You're defending him? He what, Alyssa?" Keith

asked, slapping her hand away from him. "You sleepin' with *this* fool?" He pointed towards the naked man. "I'm outta here! You can have her!" he snarled, giving Alyssa a once-over before storming out of the bathroom, nearly bumping into a bewildered Troi.

"W-what?!" Alyssa yelled, clearly confused by his sudden turn on her. "Keith, wait!" she called, clutching the towel and running after his retreating back.

"Leave me alone, Alyssa. I know what I saw! He yelled, spinning around to face her. "After all that I've done for you, and this is how you repay me? It was me who swooped your pathetic behind from that antique shop you called a job and introduced you to more upscale clients than you could possibly imagine! And you do this to *me*?" He waved his arms hysterically.

Alyssa felt anger rising in a way that she hadn't quite experienced before. Typically, she was able to swallow it, but with each passing moment, it was bubbling more and more in the pit of her stomach. And then, it came rushing forward, totally out of her control. "*I* didn't do anything to *you!* And I think you give yourself far too much credit. Let's not forget that it was me who courted and designed houses for every single one of your clients! On top of that, I stayed with you every time you lied, every time you cheated, every time you didn't come home when you said you would! It was *me*! *Me! Me!*" she clenched the towel until her knuckles had turned red.   "If I wanted to cheat, I would have already. Lord knows I've had far more opportunities to do so before this week, and considering all that you've put me through, I might even go so far as to say I deserve to cheat!" She stood with her feet planted firmly on the ground, her breast heaving up and down in an upbeat, uncontrollable rhythm.

He stepped towards her, bringing his face mere inches from hers. "If you ever raise your voice at me again," he whispered, "it will be the very last time, and you will lose every single client you've ever had or thought to have." He grabbed her chin, firmly tilting her head backwards. "Do you understand me?" His eyes peered deep into hers, his threat crystal clear.

She felt her resolve melting, a familiar picture of her mother and father flashing in her mind. She shook her head, hoping to lose the image. "I-I'm sorry," she mumbled, her eyes lowering to the floor.

He rubbed her chin with his thumb. "Good girl," he cooed, pulling her into his arms. "I'm sorry, baby. I shouldn't have accused you." He pulled back to stare into her face, his hands still wrapped firmly around both of her arms. "I should have known better than to think that you would ever put what we have in jeopardy, especially with the likes of Keshawn," he snarled. "Now, I'm going for a walk. You'll wait for me?"

Alyssa nodded her head stiffly, pulling the towel up to her chin, feeling more and more like a chastised child.

"Good. Be back." He swatted her hips and sauntered off with his hands in his pocket before turning and calling back to her. "You can lose the towel when I get back." He winked at her and retreated.

Alyssa shook her head in disbelief. In just a matter of minutes, he had managed to accuse her of cheating, demean her beyond measure, anger her, threaten her, rescind his accusation, and still leave her with an aching need deep in the pit of her stomach. How does he do that? Every time? And why do I keep falling for it?

Chapter Thirty-One

Troi

Brandon turned glassy eyes on Keshawn. "Get out, now," he growled, clenching his fists by his side.

"Mane, let me talk to my f—," Keshawn started, exiting the shower with a towel hanging loosely about his hips.

Brandon's eyes shot daggers into Keshawn, sending a clear message that damage would be imminent if he didn't comply.

Keshawn shook his head and scooted past them, clinging tightly to the towel. Once near the door, he looked as if he wanted to say something to Troi but thought twice upon seeing Brandon's clenching jaw, leaving the room instead.

"Are you okay?" Brandon asked, his shoulders relaxing.

"You know, what?" Troi sighed heavily, mustering up a genuine smile. "I really am. Whether you knew it or not, I was already done. This just solidified it for me. Keshawn hasn't been the man I met for a while now, and if this is what he wants in a marriage, I'm clearly not the woman for him either."

Brandon grabbed both of her shoulders, forcing her to look up at him. "It's me, Troi. You can tell me how you really feel." His frown lines clearly displayed his concern. She knew that he wouldn't leave her alone until he was totally sure.

She laid her hand on top of his, patting it gently. "While it's embarrassing to some degree, I'm fine, B."

He stared back at her for a long time before finally deciding to accept her answer. "Okay, well, how do you want to play this? You plan on leaving tonight, too?"

"Absolutely not!" she exclaimed. "For one, I did absolutely nothing wrong, and on top of that, despite the fact that my mom is in charge, I feel like I was really making progress in each of the sessions. Why do you think I'm not a complete mess right now?" She chuckled nervously. "I've really been able to put things into perspective, when before I was so crowded by Keshawn and my past problems with commitment that I gave myself little thought. And when I did, he made me feel so guilty. This week, I wasn't burdened by that. So, I'll be doggone if Keshawn monopolizes this, too!" Anger and determination flashed in her eyes, as she looked off into the distance.

"Alright, then, Ms. Woman Thou Art Loosed," Brandon chuckled, waving his hands and rolling his neck sarcastically. "In the words of Iyanla, ain't nobody gotta fight you for yo' healing!" He howled with laughter while dragging her out of the bathroom. "Feel up to a game of tennis?"

"Sure!" Troi swatted his arm playfully, a feeling of rejuvenation suddenly coming over her. Passing by their conjoined bedrooms, she spotted Keshawn piling his suitcase high with clothing.

She didn't say it to Brandon, but she had suspected cheating on Keshawn's behalf several times. However, she had never been the snooping type. She'd never gone through his phone or even questioned him about his whereabouts. It just wasn't in her nature; yet, recently she'd felt the need. She didn't like it. She'd always been called a hippie, just gallivanting through life as if skipping, but lately, everything had felt so heavy, so mundane, so Keshawn.

"Hey, Brandon?" She stopped suddenly, grabbing his arm. "What do you say if we throw a nice little soiree tonight instead, you know, just with the other couples; we can grill some food, play some music by the pool, just hang out?"

Brandon thought about it for a minute. "Let's do it," he agreed, taking her arm and steering her towards the kitchen.

Chapter Thirty-Two

Rosalyn

"And you believed her?" she asked breathlessly in between kisses.

"Well, yeah," Keith replied, placing a trail of kisses on her neck. "Would *you* want him over me?"

Rosalyn only thought about it for a millisecond before meeting his heated kisses with a few of her own. "Absolutely not," she giggled, as his lips taunted her ear.

"What I thought," he panted, smiling against her ear. Rosalyn was everything Alyssa wasn't, a Tasmanian Devil, just powerful and unafraid. In the past few days, he'd found himself enthralled by her, and when she wasn't around, he was thinking about her. That along with her promised connection to Brandon Lowe was enough to place her at the top of his roster.

Rosalyn could see it in his eyes. He'd never be completely satisfied, and surprisingly, she found that quite sexy. He'd never demand of her more than he, himself, was willing to offer. Without question, she'd met her match, one that she didn't even know she'd needed. She didn't have to pretend to be someone else; he knew exactly who she was and accepted her in spite of it. In fact, he complemented her immensely. This both pleased and frightened her.

She thought about the first time she'd felt this way, so totally out of control, but empowered. She'd been seventeen and yet again, her drunken mother had blackened her eye, voicing her opinion that Rosalyn would be nothing. Only this time, she had every reason to believe it; she'd just told her parents she was six weeks pregnant, which had caused her mother to tear their quaint townhouse upside-down in rampage. Rosalyn had curled up in the corner of the living room, as her mother swore to make her have an abortion as soon as possible, her father sitting by quietly.

Ultimately, she'd followed through on her

promise, sending Rosalyn to an abortion clinic alone as not to tarnish her budding reputation with Chicago's Black elite. It had been the scariest moment of Rosalyn's life, and she made a vow that if she made it through the procedure, she would never return to her parent's home.

Luckily, she'd survived and found herself walking downtown with an appetite and only twenty-seven dollars in her pocket. She'd decided to grab something to eat and finally found herself planted on a park bench, where she'd been approached by none other than Madame De'Leon, who promised to teach her the trade of being a well-paid mistress.

Madame De'Leon had taken her home, transformed her appearance, and taught her the mannerisms befitting of one of Chicago's most sought-after mistresses. By the end of next day, she'd made upwards of a thousand dollars without having to remove her clothes. She'd learned how to finesse a man's ego with the upmost delicacy while, also, tickling his fancy, suggesting that she could fulfill any fantasy he'd ever dreamed of. Madame De'Leon spoiled her and treated her like a daughter.

She'd quickly become one of Madame De'Leon's

most successful proteges before the woman's untimely death, which had led to Rosalyn seeking a fresh start in Atlanta and leaving her family in her rearview. She'd been on her own ever since, with no regrets. Nowadays, when the Chicago area code registered on her phone, she felt absolutely nothing. But Keith made her feel again; she needed to get away from him as soon as possible.

Chapter Thirty-Three

Maliah

"Troi, girl, this was a really good idea," she said, snapping her fingers to an old Jaheim cut. "This was exactly what we needed right, baby?" She called out to Mike.

Mike smiled at her over the top of the grill. "Without a doubt!" he yelled back, winking at her.

Maliah removed the sheer shawl that had been draped about her hips, revealing a black one-piece swimsuit with cut-outs just above her hips. She knew it was a risqué compared to everything else in her closet, but she was done hiding.

"Girl, you look good!" Troi explained, giving her an exaggerated once-over. "You better put that shawl back on," she said, peeking over invisible glasses. "Mike looks ready to leap over that pool." She laughed loudly, nodding towards him.

Maliah glanced over her shoulder to find Mike giving her a heated stare, his mouth hanging open. She blew him a kiss, which he caught and placed over his heart before twirling his finger in the air. She looked around before twirling dramatically, thankful that Brandon and Troi had disappeared into the kitchen.

Mike howled at the moon, sending them into a fit of laughter.

"What's so funny, y'all?" Brandon asked, sipping from a tall, virgin daiquiri and throwing them each an inquisitive look as he closed the patio door.

"Um, nothing," Maliah said, accepting one of the glasses and grinning at Mike.

With the dynamics of their relationship slightly shifting, her newfound confidence allowed them to be more playful rather than burdened with such heavy conversations. A weight seemed to have been lifted, leaving her floating on a cloud. She hadn't felt this way since college.

She sipped from the glass while staring back at the looming house, noticing Alyssa's bedroom light on. She had only heard the commotion earlier but had ran into Keshawn, who brushed past her with his duffle bag before jumping in an Uber. Whatever had happened, she just couldn't see Alyssa putting her relationship with Keith in jeopardy. She practically worshipped him. Although Maliah couldn't understand why. She wrapped her shawl around her waist again and headed towards the house, hoping to convince Alyssa to come out.

She tapped on the door softly before twisting the doorknob. "Alyssa?" she called, tiptoeing into the bedroom. "It's Maliah."

The heap of covers moved slightly on the bed, as Alyssa peeked at her. "What is it?" the woman groaned, pulling the covers back over her head.

Maliah walked to the side of the bed, standing over her. "I just came to check on you is all," she said softly.

"I'm fine," she mumbled. "Please leave."

Maliah settled into the closest armchair adjacent to the bed. "Well, you don't seem fine. We're having a little backyard fun if you want to get out the house for a minute." She attempted to pull the covers from over the woman's head, only to have them snatched right out of her hands. "Look, I don't know what happened, but whatever it was can't be that bad."

"That bad?!" The woman groaned, yanking the comforter from her face. "He accused me of cheating!"

"Who? Keith?" Maliah asked, crossing her legs at the knee and shifting in her seat uncomfortably.

"Yes, Keith!" She placed both hands on her forehead, clearly becoming more flustered. "He accused *me*!"

"Well, was this the first time?"

"Of course it was. I've never even considered cheating on him, but it was so easy for him to accuse *me* today."

Maliah tilted her head to one side. She knew that she should tell her about seeing Keith and Rosalyn leaving the poolhouse the other night, but she and Alyssa weren't friends. And considering the pedestal she'd placed Keith on, Maliah couldn't be sure that Alyssa would believe her. But she would want someone to tell her if Mike had been unfaithful.

"I gather that he's been unfaithful to you before. So, why do you think he'd be so quick to accuse you?" The woman looked back at her with a puzzled expression. "Can I talk to you like a friend?"

Alyssa slowly nodded her head, her hair in

disarray against the pillow. "Please, I could use a friend right now. Ever since I've been with Keith, I haven't had very many."

Maliah's heart went out to her. She knew controlling when she saw it, and Keith might as well be the poster child. She was obviously looking at a woman who had been conditioned into submission, which was something she saw often, even with the students she counseled. She knew that this wasn't something that happened all of a sudden; it came from years of experience, sometimes even childhood. She could see that being the case for Alyssa.

She leaned forward, her elbows resting on her knees. "From one friend to another, I'm going to tell you that if a man accuses you of cheating, it's probably because he's guilty of it himself."

Alyssa blinked several times, scooting up with her back against the headboard. She seemed to be looking through Maliah. "You know, I think you're right because just as fast as he accused me, he was quick to dismiss the whole idea."

Maliah smacked her lips. "Exactly. It's manipulation, and I've dealt with enough men both personally and professionally to know what that looks like. He makes you feel guilty by accusing you and suggesting that you shouldn't have put yourself in the predicament but then dismisses it or forgives you so that you end up feeling indebted to him. It's all part of the game."

Alyssa nodded, a forlorn expressed etched across her face. "That's exactly what he does and not just in this situation. He's always trying to make me feel like I owe him." She swept her arm across her face, wiping away tears and attempting to block out Maliah.

Maliah moved to the corner of the bed, grabbing the woman's hand. "Look, you don't have to feel ashamed for loving someone. That's what you're supposed to do, but it's up to you whether or not you allow him to take advantage of your love. You get to decide what you deserve. At the end of the day, you want a love like *His*, and I'm not talking about Keith's. I'm talking about that GOD kind of love, that won't hurt, manipulate, or leave you kind of love. That forever kind of love. I'm almost positive that's what Pastor Moore has been trying to get us to see all week; that God can heal our insecurities and show us real love while, also, helping us love ourselves. You know what I mean?"

Alyssa placed her head on Maliah's shoulder. "Thanks, Maliah," she sobbed.

Maliah placed her arm around Alyssa, offering what she hoped would be soothing words of encouragement. She saw herself in Alyssa, that whole being so insecure that you need someone else to validate you. She might have just met her, but she *knew* her. But she, also, knew that until Alyssa became fed up with the cycle of manipulation and verbal abuse, it would only continue, and her state of mind and confidence would continue to deteriorate.

Maliah patted her arm. "Now, you cannot stay in this room, especially not with some of the best virgin daiquiris and ribs waiting for you by the pool," she chuckled, pretending to lick her fingers.

Alyssa chuckled, "Okay, let me get dressed." She rolled out of the bed and strolled to her dresser.

Maliah headed towards the door, pausing with her hand on the doorknob. "Alyssa, you may not see it right now, but you can make it without him. If you look at things differently, you've already been doing just that." She threw the woman an encouraging smile, before exiting the room.

Chapter Thirty-Four

Alyssa

"Do you mind if I join you?" she asked, motioning to one of the outdoor chairs.

Troi looked up from her plate of barbeque and beans. Nodding at the chair, she said, "Help yourself." She scooped a spoonful of beans and stuffed them in her mouth.

Alyssa settled into one of the straight-backed wicker chairs, sitting her glass on the table. She leaned backwards, looking up at the night sky. "It's really nice out," she said, exhaling slowly.

"Yep," Troi drawled, her eyes fastened on Alyssa. "So, are you going to explain that little scene in the bathroom, or are we just gonna sit here pretending like it didn't happen?"

Alyssa blinked several times, taken aback by Troi's frankness. She'd viewed Troi as rather bohemian, a natural free spirit who avoided confrontation at all costs, but apparently not tonight. Alyssa couldn't blame her; she only wished she'd done as much when she had learned about Keith's affairs.

She cleared her throat. "Keith cheated on me more times than I should've allowed. That's not even counting the affairs I know nothing about," she chuckled nervously, shifting in her seat when Troi leaned backwards and crossed her arms, clearly growing tired of the run around. "M-my point," she stuttered, "is that when I found out about each affair, I was devastated. Each time it became easier to accept, but it didn't hurt any less. I know that kind of hurt, Troi; so, please believe me when I say that I would never want to be the reason for another woman's pain. That's not who I am," she said, laying her hand on top of hers.

Troi stared at their overlapping hands for a while before placing her other hand on top of Alyssa's. "I believe you," she said, the corners of her lip turning up into a smile. "Once I thought about it later, I just couldn't believe you would do that. So, we're good."

Alyssa heaved a sigh of relief, clutching her heart. "I'm so glad to know that. I didn't even want to come out here tonight because I thought you'd want to kick my you-know-what." She sipped from her glass, finally feeling her heart slow its quickening pace.

Troi squealed with laughter. "Noo, you didn't think that!" She swatted at Alyssa's hand. "That's not even my style. I'm not about to fight over a man."

Alyssa laughed, shifting in her seat. "I'm glad you're not, but I am very sorry for what happened," she said, sobering and looking Troi in her eyes.

Troi waved her off. "Girl, it's all good. It only sped up the inevitable. There was no way that me and Keshawn would make it down the aisle, especially not after this week. Call it a much-needed re-awakening."

"Right," Alyssa said, "I think we've all had a few of those this week. But, um, what made you think I wasn't that kind of woman anyway."

"I haven't seen you have eyes for anyone but Keith. You seem extremely devoted to him."

Alyssa's eyes lowered to the table. "Yeah, to a fault," she muttered. "Anyway, I'm glad you—Did you hear that?" She turned in her chair, listening for the sound of movement. After a while, she heard what sounded like muffled voices. "Where's that noise coming from?" She and Troi stood, glancing around the backyard.

"Brandon," Troi hissed, waving him over. "We here some voices on the other side of those bushes." She pointed towards the brush, attempting to keep her voice at a whisper.

Brandon moved from his seat beside Maliah while signaling to Mike, who grabbed one of the metal skewers and tiptoed towards the noise. "It's coming from the poolhouse," Brandon whispered, signaling for Mike to move to the other side of the door.

Brandon pressed his ear against the door, the voices becoming clearer. "Rosalyn?" He yanked the door open, with Mike following closely behind him. He wasn't sure what had come over him, but one minute he was surprised and the next moment his fist was slamming into Keith's shocked face.

Hearing the turmoil and the sound of a woman screaming, Alyssa and Troi ran towards the poolhouse.

"Brandon, stop!" Troi yelled, attempting to pull him away. She wasn't sure how long it would be before Keith lost consciousness. "Mike! Help me!"

She shrieked, running her hand through her hair anxiously.

Mike held up both hands. "I'm not in this one. The man deserves what he's getting." He leaned nonchalantly against the doorframe, blocking Alyssa's view.

It was the sound of Rosalyn begging and pleading with Brandon that made Alyssa finally climb the stairs, ducking under Mike's arm.

"Alyssa, don't," Troi warned, attempting to keep her from entering.

But it was too late. She'd already seen Rosalyn's naked body as she clamored for Brandon's arms, attempting to put herself between Brandon and a very naked and bloody Keith. Alyssa stood there in utter disbelief as Brandon pummeled Keith.

"Alright, alright, Brandon," Mike said, brushing past Alyssa and helping Troi pull him off Keith, who looked to be unconscious or heavily dazed, Rosalyn weeping by his side. "That's enough, man. You're gonna kill him if you don't stop," Mike warned. "Come on." He and Troi eased Brandon out of the poolhouse. He was still panting, his eyes wild and furious.

Alyssa stood over Keith and Rosalyn. "You two are perfect for each other," she scowled, removing her ring and throwing it on Keith's heaving chest.

Troi returned, placing her arm around Alyssa's shoulders and steering her pass Maliah, who had just entered, a gasp leaving her lips at the sight of the pair. Troi turned suddenly, addressing Rosalyn. "I'm sure you don't have to guess, but the wedding is off. I better not ever see you around Brandon again. Otherwise, you'll end up looking just like your new boo."

Alyssa allowed Troi to guide her down the steps, Maliah following closely behind. Once settled in the living room, the two tended to her as she wept uncontrollably, Troi wiping her tears with Kleenex and singing softly while Maliah held her hand, assuring her that everything would be alright.

For the first time, Alyssa knew why her mother stayed with her father. It wasn't because he was a provider or she feared raising her daughter in a broken home; it was because she hadn't envisioned her life any other way and being forced to do so was far more painful than all of the affairs combined. Even worse, it was a harsh slap in the face as she realized that she had played a supporting role in her own heartbreak. She hadn't even shown up for herself. Now, she was willing to face it head-on, something her mother had never possessed the strength to do but had always encouraged her to accomplish. These tears didn't just belong to her. *I finally understand you ma,* she thought.

Day Four

Chapter Thirty-Five

Pastor Charlotte Moore

"I would like to welcome each of you to the commitment ceremony, which will close out the retreat. I would also like to welcome my husband, Minister James Moore, who will help me as we close out. She motioned towards the man entering the room, who waved at each of them before affectionately hugging his wife, their hands remaining intertwined even after they had separated.

Charlotte glanced over at her handsome husband, thanking GOD that it wasn't too late to start mending what she had so terribly broken. She had become so wrapped up in shepherding her flock that she had neglected many of her wifely duties. Initially, James had willingly picked up her slack, but after almost a year of putting everyone before him, he'd grown weary, allowing the wedge between them to grow wider with each passing day. However, in the past few days, she'd went on a hunt for her husband's heart, and while they had some work to do, she was confident that they were well on their way, with the Lord's help.

She smiled over at him, at the feel of him squeezing her hand. "I understand that there was an incident last night," she said, making it a point to look at Brandon, who had a few bruises on his face but nothing in comparison to what she'd heard about Keith's conditions. "So, I understand that three of you are here alone; therefore, we will have to tweak the commitment ceremony just a bit to accommodate you because I still believe that you all have made some tremendous progress despite yesterday's events."

She scanned the five faces standing before her, all of them filled with hints of pity. "To Troi, Brandon, and Alyssa, I encourage you to keep your heads held high. I've spoken to each of you individually, and I know that none of you deserved what happened. God has greater in store for you."

She turned to James. "Honey, do you mind wheeling the water bowls out for me?"

"Not at all," he said, kissing her hand and strolling towards the cart holding five large bowls filled with clear water, each bowl littered with a different kind of flower. He wheeled them towards the group, as the others looked on in bewilderment.

"Okay, Ladies and Gentlemen, I'm going to ask you to remove all shoes and watches and unfold the towel at your feet." She watched in silence as each person did as instructed. "Okay, babe, I'm going to need your help," she said, grazing James's arm. "I'd like for you to place the bowl with the Jasmine flowers at Maliah's feet." She grabbed Maliah's hand, as he placed the bowl on the ground. "My dear Maliah, the Jasmine flower is known for its uniqueness and beauty. I pray that you always remember that God made you in His image; therefore, you never have to wonder if you're beautiful because the creator made you. Give God those insecurities whole-heartedly and watch how He will show up in your life, and even in your relationships." She hugged the woman before moving over to Mike.

"James, can you place the bowl with the Dahlias

in front of Mike, please?" She looked up at Mike, her lips sliding into a smile as she grabbed his hands. "You possess great dignity and strength. You are well on your way to being a man after God's own heart, but you must develop more patience and hold on to your values. The Dahlia is characterized by all of these things: strength, patience, dignity, and core values. Even more, in times of trouble, hold fast to God's unchanging hand, and you will get through it." She squeezed his hand before moving to Troi, her hearting swelling immediately.

"Oh, my Troi," she cooed, pulling her into a warm embrace. "My free-spirited daughter Troi," she pushed her hair behind her ears, the tears gathering in Troi's eyes. "You are like the Lisianthus flower, which varies in its color. It might be pink, purple, or even a mixture of the two, and it's known for its outgoing nature. It has an unfair reputation of being finicky, but in actuality, people only think that when they haven't taken the time to learn about this beautiful flower. That's why they cannot understand its difference. You, my Troi, must get to know God on a much deeper level, and He will help you become reacquainted with yourself, understanding that you have been given many gifts that no one can suppress. To know you is to love you, and anyone who says differently isn't worthy of your time." She squeezed her hand before moving over to Brandon.

He could hardly look at her, his eyes averted to the ground in shame. She bent down until she made eye contact. "This will be really hard if I can't see your eyes, Brandon." He raised his head, dragging his eyes upward until they locked with hers; she could see moisture gathering on the brims of his lower lash line. "Hold up your hands," she instructed. He complied, lifting his hands until they were just near his face. "You see, you've always had a gentle soul, could barely harm a fly, but your hands tell a different story at the moment. There is some unresolved anger issues that you must address, many of which stem from your childhood." She grabbed his hands, pulling them down by his side.

"You, my child, have been given the Sedum flower, which is a symbol of peace, tranquility, and endless love. The Sedum typically stores water in its leaves and stems in anticipation for hard times ahead, and that's exactly how you've lived your life. You're so worried about the what ifs and possible disruptions of your peace that you avoid taking risks, and cling tightly to things and people who present themselves as loyal, when in actuality, they are using you. It's time to heal, my dear, and with God, you will not only find inner peace but, also, a partner who truly loves you." She pulled him towards her and embraced him before, finally, reaching Alyssa.

Alyssa was already crying, her shoulders trembling with emotion. "Oh, Alyssa," she said, cupping the woman's face. "You have made such progress this week, and I hope you've realized that you are stronger than you give yourself credit for. Today, I have assigned you the Protea flower, which is known to represent transformation and courage. This week you've started the transformation process, and with great courage, you will continue on your journey and see just how much of an amazing woman you are and can be." She pulled her in for a hug, surprised by Alyssa's strong hold around her waist. It was as if she was holding on for dear life.

Charlotte knew that it would take time for Alyssa to adjust to a life without Keith; even more, she didn't trust herself, which had been a major reason for her dependency on others to make decisions on her behalf. Charlotte ended their hug, still holding her hand. "Trust yourself and stay with God always, not some days, but every day. He provides he ultimate guidance."

Alyssa nodded her head stiffly. "Yes, ma'am," she sputtered.

Charlotte stepped back, making eye contact with each person. "Now, this doesn't mean that this is the end. Of course, we still have church at least twice-a-week, but you can also participate in weekly therapy sessions, workshops, and any of our auxiliary programs." She smiled at each of them.

"Now, we're going to start the cleansing ceremony, where we will ask God for the removal of all impurities and hurt and for the renewal of your minds, bodies, and spirit. Please bow your heads as James leads us in a word of prayer." She nodded at her husband, who led them in a short prayer.

At the conclusion of his prayer, he poured small droplets of oil in each bowl.

"Alright," Charlotte said, "First, I would like for you to kneel and cleanse your hands in the water, rubbing your hands while asking God for the deeply embedded desires of your heart." She walked around them, touching each of their shoulders as they mumbled to themselves. "In doing this, you are making a step towards being made new, forgiving your pasts and restoring hope for your futures. You are making a vow that God is the author of your life, and He knows what's best. You are agreeing that you will allow Him to lead you and do His will, not yours. You will allow Him to ordain your professional and personal lives."

She stopped behind Alyssa, who was rubbing her hands vigorously in the water. "Now, I ask that you rise, and we will proceed with the washing of your feet. We know that Jesus washed his disciples' feet as a sign of baptism, but also showing His humility, servitude, and selflessness. These attributes are necessary in life, whether you're joining in Holy matrimony or not." She made it a point to make eye contact with each of them.

"Now, James and I will commence with the washing of your feet to exhibit these same qualities, in hopes that you will also demonstrate these in your daily lives. It's the final phase of our cleansing process and represents you being rededicated back to Christ. May you never be the same." She kneeled in front of Mike, as James began the spiritual washing of Maliah's feet, each of them saying a silent prayer as they worked, until alas, all had been washed.

"Now," Charlotte said, drying her hands, "it is time for the recommitment phase. I will start with Maliah and Mike." She stood before them. "If you both wish to recommit to each other, I ask that you please turn to each, grab each other's hands, and express your solemn vow one to the other."

Mike turned slowly and reached for Maliah's hand. She stared down at it before looking up into his eyes.

Charlotte could feel her heart pounding. She assumed they would stay together, perhaps, she'd been wrong.

Maliah's lips slid into a grin. "Of course, I recommit to you." She linked her fingers between his.

Mike clutched his heart, heaving a long sigh of relief. "Woman, you're trying to give me a heart attack. Come here." He pulled her in for a quick hug before holding her at arms-length. "Maliah, this week has brought a lot of deep reflection and insight for me. Our flaws were on full display, and you're still here by my side. But I'm not recommitting to you solely because of your devotion to me but simply because your imperfections are perfect for me. Even with them, you are still the best woman I've had the pleasure to date. So, if you'll have me, I'd still like to marry you, and I promise that for the rest of our lives, I'll protect, support, serve, and love you with the love God has given me." He kissed her hand and wiped a traveling tear from her face with his thumb.

"Sounded a lot like your proposal," Maliah laughed, wiping her face with her inner arm. "Whew, okay." She shuffled her feet excitedly. "Mike, I would like to recommit to you today, and I promise to always communicate with you and to love and support you. I vow to refrain from jumping to conclusions and to always give our marriage a fighting chance. I can't wait to spend the rest of my life with you." She cradled his face in her hand, as he kissed her inner wrist. *I love you*, they both mouthed.

Charlotte joined the others in a loud round of applause, willing herself not to cry. "Okay, now, Alyssa, Brandon, and Troi, you all are technically single at this moment, so I would like for each of you to make a statement of recommitment to yourselves."

"I'll go first," Alyssa volunteered, raising her hand. Charlotte motioned for her to proceed. "Well, in light of everything I've experienced this week, I would like to officially commit to following Christ and falling in love with myself and not riding in the backseat of my own life." She quickly swept her hand across her face, wiping away tears. "I haven't been sure of myself in — well," she shook her head, "I don't think I've ever been very confident. I've always felt the need to attach myself to someone to feel better about myself, and that has only brought me pain. So, today, I'd like to change that while, also, developing a stronger relationship with God."

Charlotte watched as first Troi, then Maliah, walked over to embrace the woman, who readily accepted their warmth. She was extremely pleased that they had found comfort in each other. "Alyssa, your recommitment was honorable, and I'm sure it traveled from your lips straight to God's ears. I'm confident that you will get there."

"I'll go next," Brandon said, clearing his throat. "I've probably been the biggest fool here." He chuckled nervously, rocking on his heels.

"I doubt that!" Alyssa snorted, joining the others as they chuckled heartily.

"Well, okay, maybe one of the biggest fools," he saluted Alyssa. "But I've found that I want an equal partner, a woman who genuinely loves me as much as I love her. I don't want to force a union that God hasn't approved. Even before my mother passed, I was looking for someone to nurture me, and at times, I've been so focused on being married and having a companion that I didn't set any expectations.

So, I guess, like Alyssa, I commit to work on loving myself, too." He linked his fingers behind his back.

Troi reached over and squeezed his arm, eliciting a smile from him.

"Well, Brandon, you definitely were committed to doing the work this week. And while I don't like how things transpired, I'm glad that you have clarity. God loves you more than enough to send you what you need. Now," she looked to Troi, "it's your turn."

Troi clasped her hands together. "Well, I would like to recommit to my passions, which are singing and the youth ministry. I recommit to not allowing anyone to hold my past over my head, and I recommit to being free, not bound to anyone. I will no longer allow anyone to suffocate me."

Charlotte beamed, "Troi, I'm pleased with your affirmation. I'm so glad that you've come to this realization and understand that with God, you are truly free indeed, anything less is not of Him." She scanned the line of people standing before her, emotion overwhelming her. "If I'm being honest with all of you, I had no idea how this week would go, but each of you showed up every day, determined to complete the tasks before you. I am beyond proud of all of you. To Maliah and Mike, I wish you a happy journey towards the wedding, and I would be absolutely honored to officiate your ceremony. Now, all of you please come give me a hug before I pray us out."

They circled her and James in a hug, giving each other words of encouragement.

Charlotte said a silent prayer:

> *Thank you, God for giving me the words to say to your people. May they utilize all of the tools and advice they've received this week, and may they always look to you for guidance.*
>
> *Amen.*

Epilogue

Brandon strolled into the dimly lit church, scanning the pews. He didn't see her.

"Excuse me, sir," one of the ushers whispered. "The ceremony's about to begin. Please be seated."

Brandon looked about the room, before taking a seat close to the entrance. He was a tad bit disappointed, as he'd been looking forward to seeing her, even though they'd already spent time together this week.

He'd taken the retreat seriously, to say the least, and he'd vowed to stay single, but going through the experience together had only brought them closer. He'd found that a great deal of what they'd been looking for in other people, they'd found in each other. He hadn't asked her to be exclusive yet, but he planned to very soon.

"I made it," Troi said, plopping down on the seat beside him. "The workshop went longer than expected, but here I am!"

Surprised, he turned to face her. "Glad you could make it. You look less boho, but nice." He grinned, nudging her with his elbow.

Troi punched him in his arm playfully before looking around. "So, where's Alyssa?" she asked. She tilted her head, looking at him accusingly. "Did you already run her off?"

"Not at all," Alyssa interrupted, standing at the end of the pew and looking down at them.

Brandon stood immediately, moving out so that she could pass. "I'm glad you made it," he said, softening.

"Me, too," she said, her face glowing, as she slid onto the space beside Troi. "Hi, lady!" she greeted, hugging her and temporarily forgetting about Brandon.

"I'm glad you remember my name considering how much time you've been spending with this guy," she jerked her thumb towards Brandon. "Me and Maliah were starting to think that you'd forgotten about us."

Alyssa and Brandon blushed, as he draped his arm on the pew behind her and planted a soft kiss on her cheek. "Yes, it's been really nice," Alyssa said, patting his leg. If anyone had told her that she and Brandon would be dating merely six months after meeting, she'd have laughed, but she didn't regret any of it, especially considering Keith's spiteful behavior lately.

"She's coming," Troi whispered, as all of the guests stood.

With soft jazz music playing, Maliah floated into the entryway, her dress beautifully draped on her body as her brother escorted her inside. Alyssa inhaled slowly, the mere sight of the bride taking her breath away. The soft glow of candlelight bounced off her dress in spectacular circles. And as Maliah passed their pew, she got a sneak peek at her delicately made-up face, which was already tear-stained.

Once at the altar and facing Mike, he removed her veil, their emotions upon seeing each other face-to-face overwhelming everyone in the room. Their deep love and devotion were evident in the gentle nature with which he held her hand and her wiping the tears from his face.

Both Troi and Alyssa found themselves crying before they knew it, laughing as they clung to each other. "We're a total mess," Alyssa whispered, chuckling.

"Not as much of a mess, as my mom," Troi said pointing towards the presiding Pastor. "She looks ready to ball up into the fetal position." They snickered softly.

"And now, it is with great pleasure that I pronounce you husband and wife. Ladies and gentlemen, please stand for Mr. and Mrs. Mike Peterson!" Pastor Moore exclaimed, wiping her own fallen tears, as her husband James climbed the stairs, pressing his handkerchief in her hand, holding her by the waist, and kissing her cheek.

They all stood, cheering as Mike and Maliah marched hand in hand down the aisle as the guests threw rice and shouted their well wishes.

Clapping as the couple passed, Alyssa and Troi beamed, both delighted for their newfound sister and sure that their own time was approaching, one perhaps sooner than the other.

A Love Like His

Want more J.D.?

Visit **www.jdparks.com** to join the email list

Or email J.D. at: **contact@jdparks.com**

Follow J.D. on Instagram: j.d.parks_author

ABOUT THE AUTHOR

Born in Chicago, IL, and raised in North Mississippi, J.D. Parks has been a strong advocate for leading a multi-purposeful life led by GOD; Hence, she enjoys exploring and combining the lived experiences of under-represented people in cross-genre fiction. J.D. currently serves as an Adult Sunday School teacher in her church and a college-level English professor at a Historically Black College in the Mid-South. When she's not writing, reading, or performing both simultaneously, she is relaxing with her family and sipping from a tall glass of strawberry lemonade.

www.ingramcontent.com/pod-product-compliance
Lightning Source LLC
Chambersburg PA
CBHW022005170626
46808CB00001B/298